JIMMY SPOON
—AND THE—
PONY EXPRESS

Other Apple Paperbacks
you will enjoy:

The Captive
by Joyce Hansen

The Lampfish of Twill
by Janet Taylor Lisle

Steal Away
by Jennifer Armstrong

The Journey Home
by Isabelle Holland

JIMMY SPOON
—AND THE—
PONY EXPRESS

KRISTIANA GREGORY

AN
APPLE
PAPERBACK

SCHOLASTIC INC
New York Toronto London Auckland Sydney

ISBN 0-590-46578-3

12 11 10 9 8 7 6 5 4 3 2   4   7 8 9/9 0 1/0

Printed in the U.S.A.   40

*For my brother and sister, cherished friends from
childhood and friends still:
Rob Gregory and Janet Gregory Coen,
and
to the memory of
Theron Dunn
Na? Dagwiship
1969–1993
A ''Sho-Ban'' Warrior taken too soon*

CONTENTS

Contents

AUTHOR'S NOTE

Jimmy Spoon and the Pony Express continues the adventures from *The Legend of Jimmy Spoon*. Both novels are fiction based on the memoirs, *Among the Shoshones*, by Elijah Nicholas Wilson. The town of Wilson, Wyoming, named for that author, is at the southern base of the Grand Tetons in Wyoming.

In the 1850s, a letter mailed from New York took six to eight weeks to reach San Francisco: First it traveled by ship south to the Gulf of Mexico, then by mule and canoe across Panama, and again by ship up to California. If a letter went by covered wagon along the Overland Trail, it could take months. People joked that news had already been forgotten on the East Coast by the time folks on the West Coast heard it.

The Pony Express began April 3, 1860, covered a distance of nearly 2,000 miles, and lasted just eighteen months. News was telegraphed from various eastern cities to St. Joseph, Missouri, where someone in a tiny office would decode the clicking, then write the message on lightweight paper and slip it into an envelope. Postage was five dollars a half ounce. The telegram — along with military dispatches and newspapers printed on special tissue — was put into one of four padlocked pouches of the *mochila* (Spanish for knapsack).

Riders averaged ten miles an hour, racing relay-style all the way to Sacramento in just ten days. Theoretically a fresh horse would be waiting every fifteen miles, a fresh rider every fifty or so. Because there was a telegraph office in Carson City, Nevada, some news could be wired ahead to California with a message that the rest of the mail was on its way.

On October 24, 1861, the telegraph wire system was completed in Salt Lake City, Utah. Though rates were high — up to seventy-five cents a word — messages now could be sent cross-country in just four hours, making the Pony Express obsolete.

WANTED: Young, skinny, wiry fellows not over 18. Must be expert riders, willing to risk death daily, orphans preferred. Wages $25 a week . . .

—*March 1860 newspaper ad*

"A whiz and a hail, and the swift phantom of the desert was gone before we could get our heads out of the windows."

—*Author Mark Twain,*
on sighting a Pony Express
rider from his stagecoach,
summer 1861

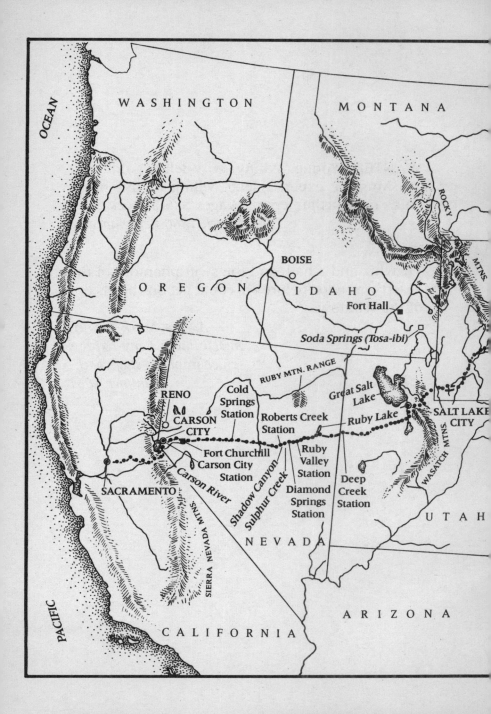

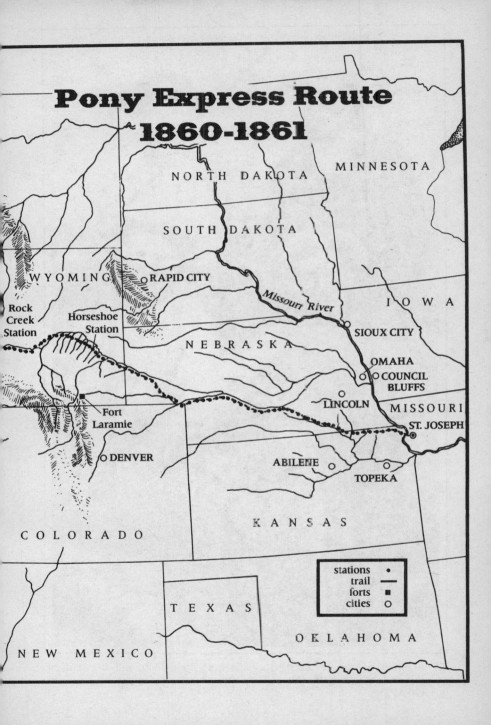

Pony Express Route 1860-1861

NORTH DAKOTA

MINNESOTA

SOUTH DAKOTA

WYOMING

RAPID CITY

Missouri River

IOWA

Rock Creek Station

Horseshoe Station

SIOUX CITY

NEBRASKA

OMAHA

COUNCIL BLUFFS

Fort Laramie

LINCOLN

MISSOURI

DENVER

ST. JOSEPH

ABILENE

TOPEKA

KANSAS

COLORADO

stations	•
trail	—
forts	■
cities	○

TEXAS

OKLAHOMA

NEW MEXICO

St. Joseph Pony Express riders: (clockwise from the top left) Billy Richardson, Johnny Fry, Charley Cliff, Gus Cliff. (Courtesy of Pony Express Museum, St. Joseph, MO)

1

ORPHANS PREFERRED

Winter sunlight slanted in through the broad windows of Spoon's Fancy Store. Jimmy gazed longingly outside at the wagons rattling along the muddy road and the men on horseback, all going someplace in the crisp fresh air. He leaned over the glass countertop where his reflection showed his bow tie was crooked again. His sandy brown hair curled above his collar, which was so stiff with starch, it scraped his neck miserably. The start of a moustache on his upper lip was the only good thing about this week.

What bothered him more than being cooped up in his father's store were the female customers warming themselves around the small iron stove.

They were his sisters' friends and they were whispering about him.

"When I get married," one of them boldly announced, "I'm going to shop here for my *trousseau*, at Salt Lake City's finest fancy store." Jimmy blushed when he heard the word *trousseau*, knowing it meant items a bride wears on her honeymoon. He looked helplessly out the window, aware that the girls watched him adoringly.

How he ached to be in the fresh air, away from the city. Instead of suffering in this store, he wished that he could be with his Shoshoni friends, hunting elk or walking in the woods with Nahanee, lovely Nahanee.

Jimmy's eyes fell on a newspaper his father had left on the counter. A headline on the front page made him catch his breath. As he picked it up, his heart began to race with excitement.

"Boy howdy!" he yelled, his voice echoing off the tall ceilings.

The girls looked up, surprised. Jimmy was usually so shy around them, he either blushed or stuttered. Never had they heard him holler.

Thinking he should explain himself, Jimmy read out loud the news that would surely captivate them: "WANTED: Young, skinny, wiry fellows not over 18. Must be expert riders, willing to risk death daily, orphans preferred. Wages $25 a week. . . .

"That's me all right!" he said. "It's for mail delivery, from St. Joe all the way to Sacramento in just ten days — ten days! — instead of six weeks. This is good news — what am I saying? — this is the *best* news, a job away from home!" Jimmy burst out with a giddy laugh, then stopped himself when he saw the girls' startled faces. How would he be able to contain himself until the store closed, another six hours away?

Lillian Zimmerman's dress rustled as she moved down the aisles toward him. Her shoes clicked daintily on the clean wood floor. She and Jimmy had known each other since childhood. If anyone would understand the reason for his new happiness, it was Lillian.

When she put her slender hands on the counter, Jimmy caught a scent of her perfume and was surprised how good it made him feel.

He felt his face get warm. "Hello, Lillian."

"Hello." She smiled at him shyly, then whispered, "Jimmy, I thought you wanted to be a captain in the army like my father."

"I do. I mean, I did. Maybe I'll do both."

"Well then, you'd better learn to dress properly. Your shirt is inside out again."

It was snowing when Jimmy hung the CLOSED sign in the window. He stepped outside, then, with the bell tinkling against the door, shut and locked it. The mud was frozen now and powdery white. A carriage with a tin lantern swinging by the seat passed quickly behind a trotting mare.

Jimmy couldn't wait to find his friends, the Cone brothers and Pen Hailey. He hurried along the planked sidewalk, his coat pulled above his ears for warmth. As he rounded the corner by the houses where Brigham Young lived with his many wives, children, and hired help, Jimmy heard shouts. Three boys burst through a gate in the high stone wall that surrounded the estate.

"Jimmy!"

"Fellas!" Jimmy swatted them playfully with the *Deseret News*.

"Can you believe it, Jim, a pony express? Know what that means? Folks'll be so happy to get their mail in ten days, the riders could end up heroes."

Heroes. Now this was something Jimmy hadn't considered, but the idea appealed to him very much. Something bothered him, though.

"I'm not an orphan," he said, as if he'd just realized this.

"That's true, Jim, but I am. So's Will here and Nick. We're orphans, sure, but ain't nobody can ride a horse good as you, Jimmy. Nobody."

"Maybe . . . maybe not. Another thing, Pa needs my help to run the store and now that I think of it Mother would never consent. . . ." Jimmy looked down. He was remembering how he'd run away from home when he was twelve and for two happy years lived with the Shoshoni Indians. When he finally returned to his mother, she was so happy to see him she had wept with joy.

Jimmy had promised her he would never again run away.

Snowflakes hissed as they drifted onto the boys' hair and thin shoulders. Their breath made steam in the cold air. The ten eastern gables of the Lion House were beginning to glow with candlelight.

Downstairs in the Beehive House there was a silhouette of someone carrying firewood to the hearth. From one of the kitchens on the estate, an aroma of cooking meat drifted out an open window.

Nick and Will, who were hungry and who were not wearing coats, began rubbing their arms for warmth. Their woolen shirts felt thinner by the moment. The cold and the delicious smell of supper made the boys look at one another, trying quickly to think of some way to convince Jimmy to change his mind.

"Tryouts are tomorrow, Jim," Pen said, knowing how much Jimmy enjoyed showing off. "One of the trail bosses from Russell, Majors & Waddell is comin' in with some wild mustangs. Y'gotta come with us, Jimmy. Pay's good. It's the same we're getting from President Young but alls we do is clean out stables, pigeon coops 'n' such that puts a boy to sleep. Pony Express riders won't be bored and they sure won't be slaves, that's my guess."

Will began stomping his cold feet and rubbing his arms faster. "Practically the whole town of Salt Lake'll be watching," he said. "They're turning Main Street into a rodeo arena come noon, snow or no snow, what d'you say?"

Jimmy's mind raced. Leaving home for a job, now that was different from running away. Surely his mother would understand. He had worked faithfully for his father for almost three years and he now had a younger brother: Little Thomas could be the one to take over the store someday.

The idea of again living in the wilderness thrilled Jimmy. He might be able to see some of his Shoshoni brothers, or at least he would feel closer to them knowing their trails were nearby. Also, there would be danger and Jimmy would be a hero. Who could resist that? He had another thought: The rodeo would be a chance to show Lillian Zimmerman that on a horse he could wear his shirt any way he darned pleased.

"Fellas," Jimmy said, giving each shivering boy a hearty handshake, "noon sounds so good t'me, I'll be there at eleven!"

2

RODEO

Piles of shoveled snow were on the shady side of Main Street where women in wool capes and bonnets began to gather. In the growing excitement, children chased each other, some swung from the damp hitching rails, other played hide-and-seek behind their mothers' skirts.

Most of the men made themselves appear important by inspecting the corral of wagons that now formed an arena in the wide street. They inspected ropes, they inspected — from a safe distance — the huffing, pawing mustangs that paced in an outer corral.

When Mr. Alexander Majors stood on a wagon seat, the crowd fell silent. He wore a stovepipe hat and long dress coat, and his beard was freshly barbered.

"Ladies and gentlemen," he yelled with raised arms. "This is not for the fainthearted nor the pale in spirit. We have wild horses and we have boys who want to ride 'em. Come April *some* of these boys will be racing across the Territory where unsavory thugs and outlaws wait in ambush, folks, where hostile Indians are looking for scalps.

"But *I'm* looking for heroes today, ladies and gentlemen, heroes who'll help deliver mail between the east and west coasts faster than ever before. Now let's see what these boys can do!"

The crowd roared with enthusiasm. The boys waiting by the horses threw hats in the air and congratulated one another as if they were already galloping across the desert. Out of nearly sixty confident boys that noon, just twenty-three would stay in the saddle long enough to buck around the ring. Only eleven of them would be hired by Russell, Majors & Waddell to be Pony Express riders on the most rugged and dangerous route of all: Salt Lake City to Reno and back.

As wranglers boosted each contestant into the saddle before opening the chute, they wondered if these boys realized what they might be getting into. There were twelve-year-olds half as tall as the horse, thin boys lighter than their sisters, boys who'd never ridden anything except a bumpy plow seat. One by one they slid off, were bucked off, or chickened out at the last minute.

By two o'clock, the Cone brothers had each

made it three times around and each survived a furiously bucking stallion. Pen Hailey made it twice with a safe leap out of the saddle. Jimmy sat on a post by the corral, calmly waiting for his turn. He was pleased to see a cluster of girls watching him from the second-floor porch of his father's store. There was no mistaking his twin sister Nan in her blue cloak and next to her Lillian Zimmerman, red-cheeked from the frosty air.

His parents were also watching with his other sisters and little brother. They waved and called Jimmy's name every time he looked up. The atmosphere was that of a holiday as most businesses had closed. The fire brigade's band played patriotic marches and Mr. Diggle put his popcorn wagon to work, filling the air with the luscious aroma of hot buttery corn.

The night before, when Jimmy had talked to his family about the newspaper article, his father's eyes lit up. With a dreamy look he exclaimed, "By Jove, son! If I were your age, I'd do it! Why, the very future of our country depends on young patriots like you." Jimmy's mother had stood quietly near the stove. He knew by her face that there were things he needed to think through, things he needed to tell her.

"James Henry Spoon!" called the voice of Mr. Majors.

Jimmy looked up. It was his turn. "Sir!" he answered. Knowing that everyone's eyes were upon him, he straightened his shoulders and, feeling a nervous twist in his stomach, took a deep breath.

He made a handsome sight. His pants were tucked into tall leather boots and he wore the red flannel shirt his mother had made him. Few knew that the bandana tied around his neck had been a farewell gift from Chief Washakie, or that a pocket inside Jimmy's vest held an eagle feather. He took another deep breath, drawing strength from the memory of how he'd earned the eagle feather. He also remembered the river where Washakie taught him to ride his first wild pony. What a happy day that had been.

The mustang stomped in its chute, enraged to be confined. Its nostrils flared when Jimmy approached, its ears lay back. The crowd grew still.

"Easy, fella," Jimmy said softly as he climbed the fence. "I'm not gonna hurt you. Easy." He reached under its belly to uncinch the saddle. It dropped to the mud. Gently he stroked behind its fuzzy ear, slipping his fingers under the harness, unbuckling it, then pulling it down over the nose so the bit could come out. Now the horse was as bare as when captured on the prairie. Jimmy nodded to the wrangler to open the gate.

"Son, you ain't on the horse, yet."

"I will be soon enough. Now kindly open it."

The wrangler hesitated. He had never seen anyone ride these horses bareback except Indians. What if the boy got hurt?

"Please, mister."

"You're the boss, sonny." He flung open the gate, freeing the powerful animal. As it bolted from the chute, Jimmy launched himself from the fence as if diving across a pond. When he landed safely on its back, a cry of relief rose from the spectators.

Jimmy laced his fingers into the tangled mane, squeezed his legs against its sides, and began leading the horse in a graceful canter around the ring. On the second loop, Jimmy slid down against its side, still holding on with his strong legs, making it appear that there was no rider. He thrust his arm under the horse's neck, pretending to fire an arrow, a trick he had learned from Nampa and the other warriors. A man tall in the saddle makes an easy target, they had taught him. This memory made Jimmy wish he were riding through a meadow and that the cheering crowd was instead his beloved Shoshoni.

As the horse neared Mr. Majors, Jimmy pulled himself up, tucked one foot under himself in a crouch, then leapt up to the wagon. With a smile, Jimmy saluted the astonished man, and jumped down. He sprinted across the arena where he caught up to the horse, grabbed its mane, then sprung up as easily as if there had been stirrups.

Pen Hailey slapped Jimmy's back in congratulations as Jimmy scraped manure from his boots on the edge of the planked sidewalk. Mr. Majors hurried over and, extending his right hand, grinned like an uncle. "Name's Alexander Majors. Where'd you learn to handle a horse like that, son?"

Before Jimmy could answer, his younger sisters and his brother broke through the crowd. The four-year-old boy holding Lucy's hand gazed up at Mr.

Majors from under his tweed cap. "Jimmy killed a bear once," Thomas said.

Annie pulled the man's sleeve, knowing he was the one in charge. "Jimmy's brave," she assured him. "He rode clear up to Fort Hall with no pants on, just his shirt and his bare behind. We saw!"

"Liar," said Emma, sticking her tongue out at her sister, then turning to Mr. Majors all polite. "He's the bravest boy there is, sir. He's Chief Washkey's blood brother, just ask Pa, and he speaks Shosho-nee as good as English."

Mr. Majors was amused by the children's reports. At the mention of the chief's name he grew thoughtful. He took off his hat and seemed to study it. "Now *there* is a man I hold in high esteem, Washakie, a man of peace. We met several years ago at Fort Hall."

Jimmy felt his throat tighten. He was proud to be Washakie's adopted brother. Hearing a stranger speak fondly of the chief made Jimmy realize how deeply he missed him.

"Sir?" he said, swallowing hard to keep his voice from breaking.

"Yes?"

"Did I get the job?"

Mr. Majors threw his head back in laughter, then reached out to shake Jimmy's hand again. "Forgive my poor manners, son. You had the job almost the moment I laid eyes on you."

3

NO CUSSING ALLOWED

By March, eighty boys, most of them under the age of nineteen, had been hired from several cities. Stations with corrals were being built every fifteen miles between St. Joseph, Missouri, and Sacramento, California. Jimmy, Pen, and the Cone brothers were assigned to the Ruby Valley Station in the Nevada desert. From there they would ride relays in either direction. Many of their resting spots would be just crude lean-tos with clearings in the dirt for them to sleep.

The morning before they were to leave, Jimmy found his mother hanging laundry on the line out back. When she saw he wanted to talk, she removed the wooden clothespin from her mouth and touched his hair in the affectionate gesture mothers have for their sons.

"Ma, I know you don't want me to go."

"True," she said. "Guess I'm afraid you'll not come back to us, Jimmy. I already missed out on some of your growin' up."

"Yes, ma'am."

"But your pa's right. You're seventeen, nearly a man. Why, someday you'll marry and be away from us anyhow." Mrs. Spoon gazed toward the towering Wasatch Mountains whose snowy ridges looked close enough to touch. The profile of her face seemed pretty to Jimmy, even though it showed the weariness of a woman who has borne eleven children. He wanted to throw himself into her comforting arms.

"I've been thinking on that, too, Ma. Mr. Majors says I'll be riding across Shoshoni trails. Washakie will be near, so will Nampa and Ga-mu. Maybe Old Mother will be traveling with them, too . . . I miss her, Ma."

Tears came to Mrs. Spoon's eyes, but she smiled. "Jimmy," she said with a sigh, "every day I thank our good Lord for Old Mother taking care of you those years, for loving you in my absence. I'm pleased you honor her."

Jimmy looked at the puddle by the well. Six ducklings splashed their wings for a bath, peeping loudly. He wished he could feel as lighthearted. "Mother, there's something else."

She looked at him. "Nahanee?"

Yes, he nodded. Words failed him now. Nearly

three years had passed since he'd seen Nahanee, but the image of that last morning kept returning to him, when the sunlight had caught the sheen of her hair, the beauty of her face. And how proudly she wore his bearclaw necklace.

Jimmy was sad to leave her. He hadn't wanted to return to his white family, but rumors of war made him think he must. Each week that had passed, he thought of her, though the memories were beginning to fade. Now for some reason, the pleasant scent of Lillian Zimmerman's perfume confused Jimmy. He longed for something he didn't understand, and this longing made him anxious to see his Indian family again.

Mrs. Spoon tenderly drew Jimmy to her, then held his shoulders. She could see the faint shadow of his mustache and how his jaw was looking more and more like his father's. The world of men and danger and heroes was not something she easily grasped. But she did understand matters of the heart.

"You'll do us proud, son, of that I'm certain." She looked again to the mountains. "Nahanee is a lucky young woman. I hope you find her, Jimmy."

After supper that evening, crowds swelled into the meeting hall to watch eleven boys be sworn in as Pony Express riders. Mormon President Brigham Young took the podium for a rousing speech. Laughter rippled through the audience as three yellow cats followed him onto the stage. They weaved between his legs and arched their backs against the tops of his boots. President Young was fond of cats and often kept scraps of dried fish in his pockets for them.

Jimmy's voice was clear and strong when he read the contract: "I hereby swear before the great and living God that while I am in the employ of Alexander Majors, I agree not to use profane language, not to get drunk, not to gamble, not to treat animals cruelly, and not to do anything else that is incompatible of the conduct of a gentleman.

"And I agree, if I violate any of the above conditions, to accept my discharge without any pay for my services." Jimmy signed the document, promising to work for one year. He then shook hands with Brigham Young, whose imposing figure and deep voice made Jimmy feel shy. He had known the president all his life because Mr. Spoon and Brigham Young were well acquainted.

Alexander Majors presented each boy with a palm-sized Bible, bound in suede. He held up his arms as if giving a benediction.

"Gentlemen," he said, "may you read these Holy precepts, treasure them in your hearts, and may they enrich your life and, as a result, enrich the lives of those around you. God bless you all. Wagons move out tomorrow. See you at sunrise!"

4

A NEW HOME

Jimmy stooped to enter the peculiar hut. It was a log cabin, but the logs were standing up like posts. Instead of windows each wall had a hole the size of a cookie, through which a rifle could point. Slivers of sunlight entered the dark room between the logs.

As Jimmy's eyes adjusted to the dim light, he saw eight bunks, a table, and north and south fireplaces. In one, a tall black coffeepot rattled over coals, and in the other was a cauldron of steamy water. The dirt floor was damp.

"Welcome to your home station, fellas," said the large man in the doorway. "Got a few weeks thereabouts before the Express starts and plenty t'do in between. Hole for outhouse gots to be dug, then

17

stable spiffed up. Your ponies'll be herded here any day now. Milo Young's the name, by the way, no relation to that pole-igamist Brigham Young. Supper's at sundown."

He hefted a juniper log that had been delivered by the wagon, then carried it on his shoulder toward a half-finished shed. Jimmy stepped outside where Pen and the Cone brothers were looking wide-eyed around them.

"Jimmy, we're plumb in the middle of nowheres," said Nick, his voice high with disappointment. He was fifteen, two years younger than his brother and Jimmy. Without speaking, they surveyed their new home.

Desert spread in every direction, interrupted by an occasional butte or low mountain range now purple in the waning sunlight. Sagebrush cast long round shadows. A plume of dust in the distance was the only sign wagons were continuing west with supplies and riders. The clink of a hammer echoed in the still air. In a corral beyond the shed a white-haired man named Mr. Tagg was nailing together a trough under the watchful eye of two gray mules.

"Well, boys," Jimmy said, picking up his bedroll and saddle, "let's make ourselves to home."

Mr. Tagg dished up stew. The crumbs in his beard meant they were having cornbread again tonight and that he'd already sampled plenty of it. He and Milo were the station keepers and while they were hard workers and satisfactory cooks, Jimmy noted that neither had taken a bath or combed his oily hair in the two weeks they'd all been under the same roof. And it wasn't for lack of water. Ruby Lake was just two miles away.

Jimmy also had learned there was a spring ninety yards north of the cabin, which explained why the floor was damp. How pleased he and the boys were to find this small oasis, shaded by cottonwoods. There was a pool, chest deep, with a clean sandy bottom and enough room for one man to float on his back. The spring was surrounded by boulders with one narrow path to carry out buckets of water for the stock.

By the cabin door a long-handled dipper hung above a barrel. Jimmy took a drink, passed it to Will, then squinted toward the shimmery horizon. Blurred images, dark blue on brown, soon became soldiers on horseback. Dust billowed from their midst like summer clouds.

When Captain Zimmerman reined to a stop, Mr. Tagg took his horse. Jimmy listened to the soldiers. The words "injun" and "murder" were spat out. An Overland Stage had been attacked by Paiutes yesterday, March 22. The horses were stolen and Henry Harper, the driver, was scalped. This happened near Deep Creek, just half-a-day's ride away. A sick feeling made Jimmy want to sit down.

"What's the matter, Jim?" Pen asked, joining him cross-legged in the dirt.

"Don't feel s'good, somehow."

"Are you scared?"

Jimmy shook his head, thinking. "Nope, I'm not scared, Pen."

The boys watched Captain Zimmerman fill his canteen by dunking it into the barrel. Bubbles rose to the dark surface. The dozen men from the Fourth Cavalry were adjusting saddles and scooping hats into the troughs to douse their heads; some rolled cigarettes or faced away to relieve themselves.

"We'll be all right, Jim, you'll see," Pen said, hoping to comfort his friend. Pen's curly blond hair was windblown and dusty. His face was sunburned, and even his freckles were pink. This was because his hat was too big and kept blowing off. For boys working in the desert, there was no shade except under a hat.

"We're trespassers," Jimmy said to Pen some moments later.

"What d'you mean?"

"That's why Paiutes are mad enough to kill." Jimmy remembered Washakie's words, how the *tybos*, white people, were moving in uninvited. How fences were blocking trails, how wagon wheels were crushing the precious camas flower. Without the flower, there would be no roots to eat, Jimmy explained.

Pen considered this. "If Indians don't want us riding through their land . . . Jim, are they really going to try to kill us? Mr. Majors said so, but I didn't believe him."

Jimmy didn't answer. He was furious at himself. *How could he have so recklessly signed up to be a tres-*

passer? He'd only been thinking of himself, how he wanted to be a hero and show Lillian Zimmerman a thing or two. He wanted to see Old Mother again and to find Nahanee. These were things *he* wanted.

He hadn't considered what the Shoshoni might think of *Dawii*, Young Brother to the chief, helping to make the country one big safe place for *tybos*. The sick feeling inside Jimmy deepened to shame. It was too late for him to back out. He'd signed a contract, taken an oath. He had promised to help see the mail through.

5

FAST AS THE WIND

Jimmy woke suddenly. Embers in the fireplaces were the only light in the small cabin. He lay in his bunk, listening. In the very far distance, a rider was approaching.

It was two o'clock in the morning, April 6, 1860. Three days earlier, a boy in Missouri and a boy in California began galloping full speed toward each other. Every fifteen miles a fresh horse would be waiting, and every fifty or so miles, a fresh rider. Somewhere in the vast Nevada desert, two boys would pass each other so swiftly, there'd be no time to even shout "hello."

This thought made Jimmy bolt upright and hurriedly pull on his pants. *Could this be the rider he was to relieve? So soon?*

Blankets were thrown back and bare feet struggled into cold, stiff boots: A rider was coming! Mr. Tagg and Will rushed outside to ready a horse, and Pen tried to boost Jimmy's courage.

"You're the best there is, Jim. No Pie-oot will catch *you*, guaranteed."

Milo poured steaming coffee into a tin cup and handed it to Jimmy with a chunk of bread.

"Mornin', son," he said, bending close. His breath stunk from an infected tooth, but Jimmy didn't mind. Despite Milo's unwashed body and unpleasant odors, he was as kind as an old grandfather. "We're countin' on you, Jim. Soon's you reach Roberts Crik Station, ride the next relay back. Mr. Tagg'll keep the coffee on, just like always."

"Thanks, Milo. I'll try my best." Jimmy drank the scalding liquid, but tucked the bread inside his shirt. He was too nervous to eat. He lifted his coat off a peg in the wall and stepped out into the cold night.

Silhouetted against the starry horizon was a small, moving shape. It rose and fell, again and again. The faint rumbling Jimmy had heard earlier was now clearly the sound of hoofbeats. A knot clenched in his stomach, a mixture of fear and excitement. He prayed Washakie would understand he had a job to do.

Jimmy was grateful for the full moon rising in the east because it illuminated the trail like a silver ribbon. *Had Mr. Majors planned it this way, so the first riders would be guided by moonlight?*

Before he could think further, the rider, a boy

named Charlie Cliff, was in front of the cabin, leaping off his foaming horse. Charlie lifted the *mochila*, which was a wafer-thin square of leather with four pockets, off the saddle, and tossed it to Mr. Tagg yelling, "Trail's clear!" This meant there were no Indians chasing him.

Jimmy's horse was rearing with impatience as Mr. Tagg slipped the *mochila* over the horn of its saddle. Nick held the halter while Jimmy swung up. Before his right boot could fit into the stirrup, the horse bolted forward and he was on his way, galloping westward across the cold night desert.

Through the thundering of hooves a wisp of a voice reached him. "Godspeed, Jimmy!" called Milo.

Jimmy's horse sped on. Moonlight behind them made it appear they were chasing their shadow. After an hour his sides ached and he was thirsty. Jimmy was relieved when ahead there appeared the dark shape of a hut. Men were leading a horse from a corral. Maybe the two minutes allowed for changing mounts would be enough for Jimmy to catch his breath.

After jumping down, he transferred the *mochila* to the fresh animal. An eager boy about nine years old pressed a cup of water into his hand.

"What's it like, Mister?" the boy asked.

Jimmy took a drink. "Trail's clear," he responded in his deepest voice. He mounted, then, smiling down at the youngster, slapped the reins against the horse's flank.

"Yee-up!" he yelled. No one saw Jimmy's grin, or knew that his heart soared with happiness. A small boy had called him "Mister" and had pulled a souvenir strand from his pony's tail.

Yes, sir, this was his kind of job.

6

TROUBLE

Roberts Creek Station was about sixty miles west of Ruby Valley. It looked like a ranch to Jimmy. A blacksmith was shoeing a mule, and several soldiers sat nearby cleaning their rifles. They all watched Jimmy admiringly as he tossed the *mochila* then walked his exhausted horse to the corral.

The hostel was spacious inside, with wide plank floors and windows with curtains. Three long tables were heavy with breakfast and the elbows of overland travelers. Voices were loud and animated. Jimmy slumped onto one of the benches, too tired to remove his boots, but not too tired to smile at those around him. He was proud that so many people waved to him and shouted, "Howdy, boy!"

On the floor next to him was a wooden box with

a blanket and a sleeping baby inside. The baby had round pink cheeks and it did not seem to be bothered by the noise.

Jimmy tasted dried blood on his lips and felt with his tongue how parched his mouth was. Riding fast for five hours, even though he changed horses three times, was harder than he had thought it would be. His legs ached and he knew they were raw in places. Remembering the bread Milo had given him, he reached into his shirt, but sweat had made the bread soggy.

A woman with strong, tanned arms set a steaming bowl of oatmeal in front of Jimmy. Butter pooled in its center, melting into clumps of brown sugar.

"You look wore out," she said to him. "I'm Mrs. Roberts and that there's baby Lucy. Me and Tom run Roberts Crik and we're proud to have you boys stoppen here. Meals are on the house." From the center of the table she took someone's plate of half-eaten bread and gave it to Jimmy. Then, searching among the other diners, she found a mug of unfinished milk. There were bits of chewed food floating on top, but Jimmy was so thirsty he drank it straight down.

He didn't remember being led to the bunkhouse or even stretching out. But someone was now shaking his shoulder, waking him from a deep sleep. In another instant he was on a horse, still groggy, but carrying the mail east under a blue, cloudless sky, the warm afternoon sun at his back.

This is the life, he thought. Cheers from stagecoach passengers rang pleasantly in his ears. Folks liked him, he was important. What he had failed to notice, however, was that the rider he replaced was pale with fright and had been unable to speak. Nor had Jimmy noticed that soldiers were forming ranks beyond the corral.

When Jimmy sighted Sulphur Creek, he was just coming around a bluff and out of a dry riverbed. Wind blew the fine alkali dust into his eyes and mouth. Its salty taste made him even more thirsty. Jimmy was glad a fresh horse would be waiting because this one was beginning to tire. It seemed odd though, that the corral was empty with no one to greet him.

"Hello?" Jimmy called. Cautiously he dismounted, looping the reins around a post. His horse drank from a large bucket of water, and Jimmy cupped a drink for himself. "Hello?" he called again.

The sudden force of someone grabbing him knocked Jimmy to the ground, but it was only a small boy whose tear-stained face pleaded silently with him.

"Whoa . . . what happened, fella? Where's your pa?"

Still clinging to him, the boy led Jimmy inside. A man sat against the hearth shivering in pain. The long shaft of an arrow protruded from his thigh. His eyes were glazed. When he saw Jimmy he tried to speak, but his voice was hoarse.

"Pie-oots," he whispered.

Jimmy noticed a figure cowering in the corner,

someone he recognized as a fellow rider. But this boy rocked back and forth, whimpering.

"I quit, I plain quit," he sobbed. "They killed Uncle, they just outright kilt 'im."

Jimmy forced himself to think. *What was he to do?* Gently prying the boy's small arms off his, he set him on a bunk and tucked a blanket around him, then hurried outside. He was shocked to see a dead man sprawled in a trough. red water seeping into the dirt. Tracks showed that one group of Indians headed north with the stolen horses. With increasing alarm, Jimmy circled the corral.

Nine, possibly twelve, Paiutes were riding east toward Ruby Valley. Toward his home station. He knelt down to feel the droppings. They were still warm. Jimmy knew this group was not too far away.

If he hurried, he might be able to skirt their trail and ride the fifteen miles to Ruby Valley in time to warn Milo and Mr. Tagg. *But what about the soldiers at Roberts Creek? Should he turn back and notify them instead?* It would be getting dark soon and the moon wouldn't be rising for several hours.

Jimmy raced back to the cabin. "This is gonna hurt," he said to the station keeper, kneeling beside him. "But it'll be quick. We gotta do it so's you don't lose your leg."

Before the man could protest, Jimmy had snapped the shaft in two and pushed the end with the arrowhead through the back of the thigh. The man's eyes rolled up and he groaned in agony.

Jimmy found a tin of salt. He pinched enough

to pack into the bleeding wound, then grabbed a small rag rug from the hearth. He wrapped it around the injured leg.

"Hold it tight till the blood stops," he instructed. Then turning to the littlest boy, he smiled. "Your pa's gonna be all right, sonny. Help's on the way."

In the instant that Jimmy swung onto his horse he decided not to return to Roberts Creek. He must warn his friends. But this made Jimmy feel sad inside. He had such understanding and love for Indian people, how could he possibly fight them?

7

A LONELY BIRTHDAY

Jimmy could see that the Paiutes heading east had ridden around the north side of a butte. He galloped south, through a sandy arroyo, then up onto a trail that looked like a long piece of string stretching through the sagebrush.

Soon enough he saw the dust of many horses to his left, their riders hidden by the powdery alkali that rose from the trail. Jimmy could tell he was gaining on them even though his path was rough with weeds and burrows.

By the time the Indians saw Jimmy, he had passed them and made it through Shadow Canyon. Now he was closing in on Ruby Valley Station, the *mochila* still safe underneath him. He felt sorry to be pushing his horse so hard. Most of all, he was sorry these Indians believed he was an enemy.

With the setting sun at his back, Jimmy's shadow spilled in front of him like a long stain. He looked over his shoulder and was surprised to see the dust moving north. Perhaps it was the approaching darkness that turned his pursuers homeward or perhaps they knew soldiers were close.

An hour-and-a-half after leaving Sulphur Creek, he saw the cabin and Milo leading a relief horse from the corral. Moments later, Jimmy dismounted and tossed over the *mochila*. He wished he were the one continuing to Salt Lake City instead of young Nick Cone.

On the warm afternoon of May 7, Captain Zimmerman rode in with bad news. While his soldiers watered their horses he cussed about the Indians.

"Bad enough about Sulphur Creek, but now Williams Station there on Carson River, it was burned to the ground," he reported. His sunburned face looked angry. "Oscar and David Williams were kilt, along with three of their men. Cold Springs Station, sure it's two hundred miles from here, but it's still our front yard 'far as I'm concerned — it was burned, too, the boss and his stable boys scalped. Those savages are dangerous, worse 'n hornets stirred up."

The Captain's saddle creaked as he stepped into the stirrup and pulled himself up. His dark blue uniform was dusty. He swigged from his canteen, then, with water dripping from his chin, yelled for all to hear.

"Until further notice, Pony riders are to stay put, no relays. Got to rebuild stations and bring in more horses, more men. The army'll escort an Overland Stage now 'n' then, but otherwise, trail's closed. Shut down!"

Jimmy was worried. "Sir," he said, shading his eyes to look up. "What if Paiutes come after *us*? What'll we do?"

"Sonny, you can shine your shoes if you want. But me, I'd keep those guns loaded and an eye wide-open. Good day!" With a crisp salute he cantered toward the corral where his soldiers were mounting.

Marks chiseled in the wall told Jimmy it was May 13, his birthday. He looked around the cluttered room at the messy beds and plates of yesterday's food. A rustle among the sacks of flour and potatoes meant desert rats had moved in and were helping themselves.

Things were not turning out the way he had planned. One week had passed since his last ride and the trail was still closed. His father's store would be more interesting than this lonely way station. He didn't like being afraid of Indians or that they were considered enemies. He didn't like how Captain Zimmerman had said to *shoot first, ask questions later*. What would Washakie think of Dawii, taking orders from such a man?

These things confused Jimmy and filled him with doubts: Maybe he shouldn't try to find his Shoshoni friends, maybe he had let too much time pass and they'd forgotten him. Or maybe they no longer cared.

Jimmy felt sad. He peered out the low doorway where he could see Will and Mr. Tagg riding the perimeter in the hot sun. Flowering sagebrush made the desert look golden and, in the sky, clouds plumed like towers of cotton. It was a lovely, peaceful day, which made Jimmy yearn for the excitement of the trail, something to perk him up.

No one at Ruby Valley knew it was his birthday, so there would be no cake or presents. Jimmy felt comforted knowing his parents were thinking of him, and when he realized he was now eighteen years old, he felt even better.

"This calls for a swim, that's what!"

At the spring he peeled off his shirt and trousers. He dunked them a few times, wrung them out, then draped them over boulders to dry.

While he floated on his back he watched clouds drift across the turquoise sky. A red-tailed hawk circled overhead in the still air, diving from Jimmy's sight, then rising again with a small furry creature in its talons.

For a moment he forgot about being lonesome. A pleasant memory made him smile. It had been a warm day like this. Along the river, tipis stood in the shade of cottonwood trees, and cooking fires filled the air with wood smoke. Jimmy had been chasing another boy above the waterfall when he saw below him a pool, deep and crystal clear.

Nahanee was bathing with her friends.

He knew he shouldn't watch, but he couldn't help himself. She was beautiful, the graceful way she braided her wet hair.

He was surprised this memory made him ache. For days now he had watched the wide sky and listened as wind rustled the desert grass. He'd sat so still for so long a yellow-backed spiny lizard had taken a nap on the toe of his boot. Jimmy gazed at the northern trails, hoping to see some of his old friends on a hunt or gathering camas roots, but the trails were empty. Perhaps it was no longer safe for them to come this far south.

Jimmy missed the way of the Shoshoni. He yearned to be with Nahanee, to laugh with her again and watch eagles nesting.

If she and the others would not be traveling to Ruby Valley, should Jimmy try to look for them anyway? Could he bear to know they might have forgotten him?

8

OUTLAWS

Day by day the desert began heating up, like a skillet on a low, steady flame. The thermometer nailed outside on the shady north wall rose above ninety degrees each noon. Wild sunflowers bloomed on the sod roof, making the cabin look as if it wore a fuzzy gold hat.

By mid-June Captain Zimmerman declared the trails passable for mail and travelers. "Not as dangerous," were his words. He did not say the trails were safe.

White-topped wagons drawn by mules and oxen once again lumbered through Ruby Valley on their long journey west. Emigrants cheered upon sighting the dust of an Express rider. For an exhilarating moment they could see the small, crouched boy on his pony, but he passed so swiftly he was gone in a blink.

It was a warm, still afternoon when Jack Slade cantered in from Deep Creek. He was one of the few riders who was older than Jimmy. For some odd reason Slade had no *mochila* and he was in no hurry.

"Salutations, gentlemen," he said pleasantly as he dismounted. "I feel duty bound to warn you that Rex Dooley and his gang are on the loose again. Till the posse catches up with them, you best stay clear of Eagle Canyon. They caused a lot of trouble for some miners thereabouts."

"What sort of trouble?" asked Mr. Tagg.

"Well, to be perfectly frank, gentlemen . . . the miners are dead."

"Is that so?" Milo exchanged knowing looks with Mr. Tagg.

"That's right," Slade answered. "Now if you'll excuse me, I must continue on my journey. I've been reassigned to Carson City Station." He filled his canteen, then, while his horse drank from the barrel, he freshened up. He ran a comb through his shoulder-length hair and meticulously brushed the dust off his sleeves. By the time he straightened his black string tie and repositioned his hat, he looked ready to dance in a saloon, not ride miles under a hot sun.

Jimmy admired Slade's gun and how his holster creaked when he moved. He wished he and the other boys could carry a six-shooter, but the weight was too much for a speeding pony; they were even told not to ride with a pocketknife.

"Well, don't worry about us, Jack," Jimmy said with confidence, even though he'd never met the outlaws. "We'll keep a lookout. Rex Dooley can't touch us. He's a baby. Far as *I'm* concerned, he's still in diapers."

The man laughed. "Those Dooley boys would hang a fool like you and enjoy it more than a birthday party. Diapers, that's good!"

Still laughing, he pulled himself up into his saddle and, without a word, whipped his horse into a gallop. In a moment he was gone.

Milo tipped his hat over his eyes and squinted toward the trail. He shook his head.

"Is anything wrong?" Jimmy asked.

"Jim," Milo said, resting a grandfatherly hand on his shoulder. "Mr. Tagg and I worked with Slade in the stockyards back in Missour-a. We were shocked when he was hired to ride for the Pony Express. Few folks realize that Jack Slade is a cold-blooded killer."

"A *killer*?"

"Twenty-two dead far as we know, and one crippled — got his leg shot off almost," said Mr. Tagg.

Jimmy's eyes grew wide. "You mean he's killed twenty-two people?"

"Yes, sir. Even cut off the ears of one fella and carried 'em around for souvenirs, mementos. Jim, if I ain't mistaken, that's Pen Hailey coming over the rise and you're next rider up."

9

RUNAWAY STAGE

As Jimmy sped westward he tried to imagine what a pair of cutoff ears would look like. Did Jack Slade keep the ears in his pocket or in a nice little case with velvet lining? Surely there would be blood and a sickening smell, much like the scalps he'd seen with his Shoshoni family. Jimmy didn't understand why men — *tybo* or Indian — would do such things.

A distant scream interrupted his thoughts. He strained to hear above the thudding gallop of his horse. Dust blew across the trail carrying with it another high-pitched scream. Jimmy was puzzled until he looked north.

Less than a mile away, a stagecoach raced out of a canyon pulled by a team of panicked horses.

It veered off the trail, bouncing wildly through the sagebrush. To his horror, he realized the driver's box was empty. With no one to stop the coach, it could crash and there would be terrible injuries.

Jimmy knew he was the only one who could help, but to intercept the team he would have to detour from his route. An unwritten code of the Pony Express was to take care of mail first, horse second, self third. A rider must never slow down for anything or anyone else.

But Jimmy couldn't ignore people in trouble. Their screams of distress worried him.

His horse was fast. In a few minutes he was racing alongside the stage. An elderly man's face appeared at the open window, and that of a small boy. The thundering of hooves was deafening.

"Help us, sonny!" the man cried above the noise.

Jimmy wanted to leap into the driver's box, but it towered above his head. Instead he slipped his left foot out of the stirrup, then his right. Now he bounced in his saddle as he drew along the rear horse. Tensing his legs and arms, he jumped, landing awkwardly on the animal's rising back. He clutched the harness without looking at his own pony, which he hoped would stay nearby. It was important the *mochila* didn't get lost.

One set of reins flapped over the horse's ears in such a way that Jimmy could reach them by inching forward. He wrapped them around his fist and, while squeezing his legs against the horse so he wouldn't fall, he pulled back hard.

"Whoa, boys!" he yelled. "Whoa!"

They continued to run. Again Jimmy pulled. Finally the lead horse responded, but it began turning left. The harder Jimmy pulled the sharper they turned. At this speed, the coach would flip over. If only he had his knife to slit the harness.

Suddenly Jimmy noticed a small figure to his right. It was a boy no more than ten years old. Somehow he had managed to crawl out the window and up to the roof of the swaying coach. He perched in the driver's box, trying to find the other set of reins. The brake lever was too low for him to reach.

"Careful!" Jimmy yelled, just as the boy managed to grab the thick leather straps. Pulling back as hard as his thin arms could and with Jimmy still pulling, the horses began to slow. In a moment they came to a stop in a spray of sand.

The door to the coach flew open and out tumbled another small boy, then his grandfather and two women, one holding a squalling infant. Jimmy was surprised there were so many children, but something surprised him more.

A girl his age, in a high-collared dress and white gloves, stepped out, opening a parasol as her foot touched the dirt.

Lillian Zimmerman. What on earth was the captain's daughter doing here? He was too astonished to speak.

"Oh, Jimmy," she cried, hurrying to his side. "I'm so glad to see you. Those wretched men — they bragged about being in Rex Dooley's gang — they shot our poor driver and they robbed every one of us of our valuables. Aunt Julia and I are on our way to Fort Churchill to see Father. . . . Oh, to think we were almost killed." Lillian burst into tears.

Jimmy felt uneasy, wanting to comfort her but not sure how. For several minutes they stood in the shade of the rear wheel, which was as tall as Jimmy. He noticed large parcels of mail strapped beneath the carriage, probably magazines and other letters too heavy for the *mochilas*. They were safe from robbers, but by the time the stage reached California everything would be soaked from river crossings.

Lillian brushed at the thick layers of dust on her dress and arranged her windblown hair. Jimmy thought she was pretty. He liked the way she smiled at him, even the way their arms bumped against each other. The nearness of her made him feel soft inside, and somehow lessened his desire for Nahanee. He didn't understand why this was.

He took Lillian's hand and as he helped her step up into the coach, he found himself flushed with pleasure. "We better get a move on," he said. "Mail's late and if we don't hurry, we'll be camping under the same stars as Rex Dooley."

10

WILD MUSTANGS

Jimmy and the grandfather drove the stage into Roberts Creek Station, arriving at sundown, the *mochila* safe on the seat beside them. A relief rider was waiting so Jimmy tossed the satchel to him. Mail was three hours behind schedule.

During the night a stable boy wiped off the coach so it was no longer brown with dust. At dawn it looked handsome with its bright red sides and gold lettering: WELLS, FARGO & CO. OVERLAND STAGE. Fresh horses flicked their tails and sniffed the cool morning air. Three new passengers joined the others.

Jimmy watched as they crowded aboard. He knew that those in the front and rear seats would be most comfortable because they could lean against the walls of the coach. Those on the narrow center bench had to hold onto leather loops suspended from the ceiling. Sitting knee-to-knee, their feet were crammed between canvas sacks and other cargo.

When the dust became unbearable for those facing forward, they could roll down the leather curtains or tie a kerchief over their mouths. Always there were arms touching arms and soon there would be the unpleasant odor of sweat and rancid breath. Drowsy heads would bump into shoulders.

Jimmy had heard of passengers going mad from lack of sleep or from other irritations. Dust. Heat. Motion sickness. Sometimes babies wouldn't stop crying and sometimes a person just talked too much.

Yes, that would do it, thought Jimmy. *Too much talk.* Suddenly he was filled with happiness. The endless blue sky reminded him of how free he was riding alone on a horse. Miles of open desert. Buttes purple in the distance. The wonderful sharp smell of sagebrush after a storm.

Cheerfully he saluted the stage's new driver as the man snapped the reins. The clopping of hooves and loud jangling of harnesses drowned out the cries of farewell. When Lillian leaned out the window and waved to Jimmy, he felt he was the luckiest boy alive.

After the noon meal Jimmy stepped out into the heat. Sand flies swarmed by the doorway, small and bothersome as ants. The blacksmith was shoeing a biting, squealing mustang, helped by three strong men. It would take them half a day to wrestle the animal down and nail the iron **U** onto each hoof.

Milo had explained that in the 1500s Spanish explorers rode these horses, calling them *mestengo*, meaning "wild." Mustangs were stocky with deep withers and broad flanks. They were especially valuable to the Pony Express because it had been learned that a grain diet gave them enough energy to outrun Indian ponies.

Just before supper, a rider sprinted into the yard and leaped off his horse yelling, "Trail's clear!" Three men restrained Jimmy's mount while another slipped the *mochila* over the saddle.

When he put his left foot in the stirrup, the horse reared and turned, swinging Jimmy out and to the side like a rag doll. He managed to pull himself up and grab the reins. The horse bucked twice, then reared again.

"This one's wild!" Jimmy cried to the blur of spectators. "How many times he been ridden?"

As the mustang bolted toward the trail, galloping full speed, Jimmy heard the stationmaster yell, "You're the first, Jimmy!"

11

AN EMBARRASSING MOMENT

On a cool September morning Jimmy relayed out of Roberts Creek. Dark clouds met the horizon and there was a rumble of thunder. When the first raindrop hit his neck, he shivered. It felt like ice.

Soon the hard-packed trail was muddy. Every few miles Jimmy shifted position in his saddle, but still his muscles ached as they had after his first ride in April. He sneezed. His fringed leather jacket felt heavy with the rain that now soaked his shirt, and his wet Levi's slipped against the *mochila*.

By the time Jimmy pulled in at Ruby Valley Station, he was chilled. How he wished he could soak in *Tosa-ibi*, the hot bubbling Soda Springs used by his Shoshoni family. This gave him an idea.

It would be several hours before he needed to

46

relieve the westbound rider, so there was time to rest. He hung his wet clothes on the rafters to dry. Still shivering, he set a tub in a corner near the north fireplace, which was warm with crackling piñon and a steamy black cauldron. Jimmy was thankful Milo and Mr. Tagg kept it filled with water and that they kept the woodpile high. It was not easy hauling logs from the hills above Ruby Lake.

The tub was actually a copper hip bath delivered by wagon from a society club in Salt Lake City. It looked like a coffee mug with its front scooped low. Jimmy could sit in it, water up to his hips, his legs draped over the sides. With his hat on his head to keep in body heat, he might be able to get rid of his chill.

Jimmy soaked luxuriously, eyes closed. The steam relaxed his aches and made him feel sleepy. His ears were so plugged up he did not hear the rumbling approach of a stagecoach. He did, however, feel a gust of cold air on his legs. When he looked up he saw Pen. He also saw Lillian Zimmerman hanging her shawl on a peg. She was chattering gaily about her visit to Fort Churchill. They had not noticed Jimmy in the corner.

Soon enough, though, Lillian turned. When she saw Jimmy's bare legs dangling over the tub, her hand flew to her cheek. "Oh, pardon me!" she cried.

Jimmy closed his eyes in despair. What was he supposed to do? He was exhausted. He had a runny nose and a terrible headache, which was why he couldn't think clearly. Yes, he was taking a bath, yes, Lillian Zimmerman was there. But the only logic he could make of that was to remember his father's stern advice:

Always stand when a lady enters the room.

With a splash, Jimmy lifted himself out of the tub, steam rising from his warm wet skin. After a few seconds of dripping on the dirt floor he realized his error and whisked his hat from his head down to his lap. Lillian's mouth dropped open. Pen immediately hid her eyes with his hand, spun her toward the door, and escorted her outside.

Miserable with embarrassment, Jimmy sank back into the tub. A few minutes later the stage pulled out and Pen returned, cold air sweeping into the room before he was able to close the door. "I'm terrible sorry, Jim," he said. "I had no idea you'd be taking a bath. Ain't she pretty though?"

Jimmy was groggy, but he managed a smile. Yes, she sure enough was.

"You gonna court Lillian when you get back to Salt Lake, Jimmy? She told me she likes you."

"I'm thinking on it. But I'm also thinking to go north come spring. Maybe."

Pen lifted the heavy pot from the coals and poured steaming water into Jimmy's tub. "To see your Indian family? What's that girl's name again?"

"Nahanee," said Jimmy. "We were good friends and I want to see her."

"But Jim, why would you think about courtin' an Indian when there're lots of girls in Salt Lake just dying for you to notice 'em? They smell good and have nice manners and being with them won't cause no controversy, if you know what I mean."

Jimmy sneezed. He lowered his shoulders into the hot water and closed his eyes. "It's hard to explain," he said with weariness. But somewhere inside Jimmy doubts were growing.

Maybe he should leave his past alone.

12

MR. LANTERN

By and by Jimmy's cold got better. Unless a rider was flat on his back or dead, he must get on his horse and go. Even though Jimmy didn't feel well, he continued his routes.

Late one chilly afternoon when he was rubbing down his horse, a Conestoga drawn by six mules stopped near the cabin. Several children peered out from the canvas cover.

"Welcome, strangers," called Mr. Tagg from the doorway. "Supper's almost ready. What we got is yours."

An assortment of young cousins jumped out of the wagon. A pretty woman with long red hair stepped down from the seat. She held an infant wrapped in a patchwork blanket. Another woman was round and heavy with child.

"Obliged," the driver said, reaching to shake hands all around. His large black hat made his eyes look dark. "Hank Lantern's the name and these here are my kin. We'll be movin' out by sunrise tomorrow if you all don't mind us bedding down in your front yard for the night."

Milo passed a cup of coffee to him. "Well, sir, that's all right by us, but it's somewhat peculiar you folks are headin' west this late in the season. The Donner Party — wasn't that in '46, Mr. Tagg? Yes? — well, they took the Hastings Cutoff this time of year hoping to make it over the Sierra before the big snows. Tragic. I never realized decent human beings could turn into cannibals."

"I heard about them. But we'll be all right, long as we don't dawdle. My brother and nine other families are waiting for us at Rag Town. We'll be all right."

While the men talked, Pen and Jimmy led the mules to the corral. They could see the women cleaning out the wagon as their children played hide-and-seek in the brush.

"Jim, don't it look like that one lady is gonna have a baby?"

"Looks that way to me."

"Well, where's she gonna have it?"

Jimmy shrugged. "Somewhere between here and Californy, I suspect."

They unharnessed the mules, spread fresh hay

TREML

for them, then saw to their water. Pen buttoned his coat against the chill and rubbed his hands together. "You ever wonder, Jim, why folks travel so far with every possession they have, just to look for a better place, not knowing for sure if there is one?"

"Seems all kinds of folks do it," said Jimmy. "My pa did, moved us from New York to Salt Lake City. And when I was with Washakie, the tribe moved all the time, but it was with the seasons and to follow game. Sometimes they came here to Ruby Valley, but it wasn't because one place was better than another."

Pen looked at his friend with fascination, wanting to hear more. "But didn't you get homesick for your own family?" he asked.

"At first, yes. But then it was as if I'd always lived with the Shoshoni. They became my family and I didn't want to leave."

Pen knew Jimmy had returned to Salt Lake so people could see he hadn't been kidnapped or held against his will. "Jim," he said, "if you liked it so much, living with the Indians, why didn't you go back 'soon as your folks saw you were all right?"

"I'm not sure, Pen." Jimmy closed the corral gate, then turned toward the cabin. Smoke curling up in the cool air smelled like supper. "I didn't want to disappoint my mother and father again, and somehow that was enough to keep me home."

"So what's holding you back now?"

"I keep asking myself that. One thing, I made a

commitment to Mr. Majors, and another thing
. . ." Jimmy sighed. His breath made frost. "Oh,
never mind. We better go warn Mr. Lantern
not to take Shadow Canyon. There're Paiutes
everywhere."

13

A MOTHER'S GIFT

Just before noon a galloping horseman appeared in the west, heading for Ruby Valley so fast its dust was far behind the pony's flared tail. Tight in the saddle was fourteen-year-old Billy Cody, one of the youngest Pony Express riders. Within minutes he drew to a stop in a spray of dirt.

"There're some crazy travelers out there," he cried, leaping to the ground. "I circled their wagon to warn the driver, but he kept going."

Billy was small and thin and looked too young to be riding alone in the vast, empty desert. He searched the faces around him for reassurance. "Can't we do something? Those folks're headed straight for Shadow Canyon and there's a war party waiting for 'em, Indians everywhere! I told the man but he just kept on going.''

Milo yanked off his hat in frustration and slapped it against his leg. "That miserable fool," he cried. "How can a man be so pigheaded plumb stupid? We told Mr. Lantern not to take the shortcut, we told him to go south of Shadow Canyon, not through it. We warned him, but he didn't listen."

Jimmy looked worried as he dipped a cup into the water barrel and offered it to the small boy. They had become friends during the brief times they shared layovers. "How'd you get through, Billy?" he asked him.

"Same as always. Laid low and beat it. Lost my hat, though. I felt it go *pow* off my head like I'd been shot. *Pow*, just like that. And it was my white straw one, too, cost me three dollars. Say, when're you up, Spoon?"

"Any minute. I think Pen Hailey's got the leg from Deep Creek. Oh, I wish he'd get here now; someone's gotta make Mr. Lantern turn around."

Nearly an hour later, Milo yelled from the corral. "Jim! You're up!"

There were shouts and a flurry of dust as a fresh horse, its westbound mail, and Jimmy raced away.

The faster his horse sped on, the smoother the ride. Jimmy felt that if he were a bird, this is what it would be like to fly. The wind in his face was cold and his hair blew loose behind his collar. He had a shoelace tied under his chin to keep his hat

on. Crouched low like this he could feel the sting-
ing ends of the mane.

He knew he could catch Mr. Lantern, he *had* to
catch him. If Jimmy could stop a runaway stage,
surely he could stop six slow mules.

But after several miles, he did not see any trace
of the prairie schooner. The trail was beginning to
narrow in its steep approach to Shadow Canyon.
He slowed his horse hoping to see or hear something, anything that would be a clue to what lay
ahead. If Mr. Lantern had made it through, then
Jimmy would need to hurry for his own safety.

The trail wound through a sandy gulch into the
canyon. Three feet on either side of him rose sheer
rock walls that at every hour except high noon cast
deep shadows. It was always cool in Shadow
Canyon.

There were fresh wheel tracks, fresh, Jimmy
knew, because the wind had not yet smoothed
their edges.

He looked up and around, fearful someone
might be watching him, waiting. When he saw the
man's hat in the dirt, pinned by a two-foot-long
arrow, Jimmy's heart sank.

It was a black hat.

Filled with dread, he stopped. Ahead, the trail
widened into a protected campsite. He knew
Paiutes hunted here and took refuge from the heat.
Desert bighorn sheep lived among the rocks as did
mountain lions and bobcats. Golden eagles nested
in the cliffs. A thin waterfall splashed down into a
clear, deep pool. To Jimmy it was the most beau-

tiful oasis in the desert, but at this moment it was the most horrible place ever.

Several yards around the bend, he saw the wagon. The mules were gone. When he saw the bodies he quickly turned away and squeezed his eyes shut. He knew from the blood and from the way they were sprawled, that all were dead. His horse snorted and began stepping with nervousness. It had caught their scent on the breeze.

"Fool!" Jimmy screamed to the cliffs. "Stupid man!" Enraged and filled with sorrow he buried his face in the long, tangled mane and wept. Jimmy was heartsick. Why hadn't Mr. Lantern listened to him? And why did Indians have to murder these innocent people?

Jimmy needed to think and to pray before he'd be able to gather the courage to bury the poor family. An unspoken code among travelers was that death would be dignified by burial, whether by friend or stranger, before vultures and coyotes took over.

Still unable to look toward the wagon, he kneeled in the sand. The mustang seemed to understand it was not to run off. It nuzzled Jimmy's neck as if to comfort him.

Above the sound of the waterfall Jimmy heard a faint cry, as if a kitten were mewing. He lifted his head to listen. It mewed again. Cautiously he stood up, tied the reins to a branch, then began moving toward a cluster of rocks near the pond. He wished he had one of Jack Slade's ivory-handled revolvers.

When Jimmy peered inside a low, small cave he couldn't believe his eyes. There was a baby, a live human baby wrapped in a patchwork quilt. It had red hair. Its cheeks were puffy from crying and its voice was so hoarse it squeaked like a kitten.

Jimmy reached in and tenderly scooped the bundle into his arms. Instantly he forgot about the horror behind him. His anger at Mr. Lantern was replaced by admiration for the baby's mother who had managed to hide her child safely. Apparently the Indians had not heard it crying.

"Easy, fella, easy." Jimmy used the same gentle words he used with horses, and it seemed to work. The infant gazed up at him. Its cries softened to hiccups.

Jimmy knew he needed to get the baby to safety. There was no time to bury the family.

He dipped his hand in the stream and let water drip off his fingers into the tiny mouth. Its tongue was swollen from thirst, but it was able to drink. Old Mother had shown this trick to Jimmy when they once found an orphaned papoose. This memory deepened the affection he felt for her.

Even though the air was cold, Jimmy took off his shirt. He tied it into a sling so the baby could ride securely against his chest. The horse was perfectly still while Jimmy pulled himself into the saddle, as if it, too, wanted to protect its new passenger.

14

ROBERTS CREEK STATION

The men who helped Jimmy change horses at Sulphur Creek were astonished to see a child wrapped in his shirt. But they cheered and threw their hats in the air when Jimmy managed, within two minutes, to return to the trail for his ride to Roberts Creek Station. Mrs. Roberts was one of the few women in the territory who had a baby and if anyone would know what to do with an extra one, she would.

The smooth rocking gait of the horse was like a cradle. The infant did not wake up until it found itself in the arms of Mrs. Roberts, with a dozen strange faces smiling down at it. Immediately its mouth wrinkled and it began to cry.

Jimmy was so exhausted he sat down on an upturned crate where he could see out the window to the corral. It was a cool autumn day. Soldiers from Major Hendrick's battalion were readying their horses for Shadow Canyon, for burial duty. They would bring back any personal items that might help them locate the baby's relatives.

"It's a boy, Jim," called Mrs. Roberts, "about five months old, same as my Lucy. Since you found 'im, you get the honor of naming 'im."

The scene reminded Jimmy of Old Mother and he suddenly found himself thinking in the Shoshoni language.

"*Ingabumbee,*" he said out loud. His beloved Old Mother would have named him Ingabumbee, Red Hair. He felt tears sting his eyes.

Mrs. Roberts returned to her work at the stove with Ingabumbee riding in her arm as if he had been hers all along. When he began to howl with hunger — a different cry than when he was startled by strangers — Mrs. Roberts tucked him under her bib apron and opened her blouse so he could nurse, his head supported in the crook of her left arm.

With her right hand she carried an iron skillet sizzling with potatoes and ham. She set it on the table, pulled a long-handled spoon from her apron pocket, then began serving the travelers. All this she did with quiet dignity.

Jimmy had seen Shoshoni women do the same. They cared for one another's children without question, nursing them while a mother slept or adopting them completely. There were no orphans among Indian people.

After supper Jimmy moved the crate he'd been sitting on and turned it over next to Lucy's box, which was near the fireplace. With the patchwork quilt he made a soft cozy cradle. He was amused to see Ingabumbee propped against Mrs. Roberts's shoulder. The baby's fuzzy red hair stood straight up, and he was looking wide-eyed around him as she stacked dishes with her free hand. She brought to the table a bowl of sweet, yellow apples.

Jimmy took the boy. He wanted to help Mrs. Roberts as he had helped Hanabi with baby Oddo and his own mother with little Thomas. They were all the same, babies were. They needed to eat, sleep, and be rocked. He knew the men in the room were staring at him, but he didn't care.

Washakie hadn't laughed when Jimmy swept out Hanabi's tipi or when he did chores that only women were supposed to do. He was proud he remembered the chief's words: "If you can do good to someone, do it. It does not hurt for us to help one another."

15

TWO SOUTHERN GENTLEMEN

One of the men in the crowded room sat by the hearth, turned toward the firelight. He was writing in a small brown notebook with a stub pencil. He kept glancing at Jimmy and Ingabumbee as if he were making notes about them. His reddish-brown hair was wild, and his bushy mustache was speckled with bits of potato left over from supper. A leather satchel at his side had the name SAM CLEMENS engraved on the handle.

The odd thing about Mr. Clemens and the man next to him was that they were wearing only their short-sleeved underwear and their boots.

Mr. Clemens acknowledged Jimmy with a nod, then cleared his throat as if preparing to deliver a speech. "You seem curious about our attire," he began. "When we left St. Joe, my brother and I could not keep the dust out of our coach. Happily there were no ladies aboard so the intelligent solution, of course, was for us to disrobe and continue the journey in our Skivvies. We are southern gentlemen on our way to Carson City. In clean clothes, the governor will not mistake us for ruffians."

The blacksmith standing at the other end of the hearth leaned forward to get a better look at them. He was a large man with thick arms. He was picking ham out of his teeth with his fingernail. "You mean you two dandies rode clear to Roberts Crik in your underwear just so's you wouldn't get dirty? Why, Rex Dooley and his gang gets a bounty for scoundrels like you!" He roared with laughter and slammed his fist onto the mantel, which prompted the soldiers and other travelers — all men — to erupt in jeers.

The noise in the room was deafening. Jimmy tensed, expecting a fight to break out. Quickly he tucked Ingabumbee into his cradle. But the Clemens brothers had taken no offense; in fact they roared and stomped their boots right along with the others. Dust from the floor rose in the smoky room.

Soon it was evident to Jimmy that the two southern gentlemen dressed in Skivvies were not gentlemen at all. They were loud and they cussed. They spit on the floor. Jimmy's eyes widened when the two began telling jokes about polygamous men in Salt Lake City. They criticized the Mormon president.

"He never paid any attention to me," Sam complained. "Brigham Young was like an old cat who looked around to see which kitten was meddling with his tail. He seemed bored with us, utterly bored."

Apparently Brigham Young had not been impressed with the brothers. Maybe he had heard them make fun of his wives, or maybe they bragged too much about their jobs in Carson City. Or maybe they had forgotten to put on their shirts and trousers.

Jimmy stepped outside. There was still a blush over the western mountains where the sun had set an hour before. The air was frosty and he could see his breath. He walked to the corral. He loved it out here, away from the noise, with the comforting smell of horses and hay.

He leaned over the rough log railing and clicked his tongue. Two mares lifted their heads, considered him for a moment, then trotted over. From his shirt pocket he took out an apple. He pressed his thumb by the stem, down, until the apple split neatly in half.

"Here, girls," he said. "Easy."

While they ate, Jimmy watched the sky. Stars began appearing in the growing darkness. *Shadow Canyon must be cold and empty now*, he thought. He felt sad about Mr. Lantern and his poor family, sad that Ingabumbee lost his mother.

Lamplight glowed from the cabin's windows. When someone opened the door, laughter swelled out into the night, then faded again as the door closed. Safe inside, the baby slept. Jimmy's spirits lifted when he realized he would be able to see Ingabumbee every time he rode into Roberts Creek. Maybe someday he would take the boy north to visit his Shoshoni family.

Old Mother would love to meet a little red-haired child, and so would Nahanee, beautiful Nahanee.

Jimmy kicked a fence post in frustration. If only he could stop thinking about them.

16

CHRISTMAS EVE, 1860

A cold wind blew across Ruby Valley. Weeds poking above the snow marked the sides of the trail. Frost stung Jimmy's cheeks, making him wish he could grow whiskers to keep his face warm. He wished he had the muskrat hat and the tall furry moccasins that his dear Old Mother had sewn for him.

Around his neck he wore a gray wool scarf that itched and, under his clothes, wool long johns, also itchy. Buckskin gloves kept his hands from freezing, but by the time he would unsaddle his horse, his fingers would be too numb to hold a soup spoon.

How grateful Jimmy was to sit in front of the fire. Snow blew in through narrow cracks in the walls, melting on the floor into small muddy pools. Often others were there, too, warming themselves between rides, sometimes new boys who'd just been hired, sometimes travelers. It was easy to make friends around a fire, as it had been around the fire in Washakie's tipi. To Jimmy, there was nothing like a cozy, warm lodge in a blizzard.

One snowy evening Pen and Jimmy wrapped bread dough around twigs and held them over the coals to bake. When done, they passed one to Billy Cody who dozed in a bunk, one to Mr. Tagg, and one to another boy named Gus. While they ate the delicious hot stickbread, Milo brought his Bible to the hearth. It was identical to Jimmy's, small as a hand, and bound in soft dark suede.

"Don't s'pose you realize this," he said, "but it's a special night. It's Christmas Eve. I'd like to read you fellas something." He and Mr. Tagg still had not taken a bath or washed their hair, but Jimmy didn't mind. They could cook and they spoiled the boys as if they were grandsons.

Milo sat on a three-legged stool, elbows on his knees. His voice was soothing as he read from the book of Luke, the story of the Christ Child, the Messiah. Jimmy felt safe and warm. He wanted to sleep.

Too soon Mr. Tagg was shaking his shoulder. "You're up, Jim. Drink this cocoa, hurry. It's stopped snowing, but the wind's pickin' up."

Jimmy didn't want to leave the warm cabin. For the first time since he took the job, he did not care if mail took ten days or ten years, and he no longer cared about being a hero. It wasn't as much fun as he'd thought it would be.

The more Jimmy thought about going out into the cold, the more unhappy he became. No wonder other boys had quit. Many hadn't been paid in months. There was never enough time to sleep or warm up or just lounge around the fire with friends. Mr. Majors had given them Bibles, but he'd forgotten they would need time to read them.

Outlaws and Indians were a hazard and so were some travelers. There were several instances where nervous emigrants fired shots at speeding ponies, mistaking them for Paiutes' ponies. Another worry was riding at night. Jimmy didn't want to admit this to anyone, but being alone in the pitch-dark scared him.

When Milo saw Jimmy's sour face, he set the Bible down and grabbed his coat off a bunk. He opened the door for Jimmy, and together they stepped out into the cold where their breath turned to frost. The black sky was alive with stars. They could hear the drumming hooves of the westbound rider, approaching fast. As a grandfather might do, Milo checked Jimmy's scarf to make sure it covered his throat and neck, then gave his shoulders a quick hug.

In the next rushing moments while Mr. Tagg caught the *mochila* and Jimmy mounted, Milo called, "We need you, son. We're all countin' on you."

In a bolt, Jimmy was off. The rush of cold air woke him completely and made him crouch close to the horse for warmth. Wind drove a chill into his arms and legs as if he'd been wearing no clothes at all, but for some reason he felt excited. The night was beautiful. Snow made the desert look like a white quilt. In the pale darkness, the trail resembled a long narrow seam running between the quilt's downy folds.

Jimmy suddenly felt privileged to be out in the cold, riding a horse under stars so brilliant he wanted to shout to their Creator with joy. The things he'd been upset about earlier now seemed small. Folks were counting on him. It was Christmas Eve and he had a job to do.

17

WAR IN THE EAST

Winter was bitterly cold.

Three Gosiute hunters were found near Ruby Lake, frozen to death and starved, apparently on their way to ask for food. During the same blizzard, Pen Hailey's horse fell in a hole and broke its neck. In waist-deep snow Pen walked the *mochila* three miles to the next station. He arrived nearly frozen himself.

Several boys quit because they decided they weren't being paid enough. Some quit because they'd hurt themselves and others quit to help finish the transcontinental telegraph. Poles were being planted west of the Missouri River at such a rate that soon wires would reach coast to coast.

In winter, loneliness was sharper. Wind howled

across the desert, blowing snow over the trail and into tall drifts against the cabin. Visitors were few. Friends were separated for days at a time while they rode in opposite directions. Sometimes a relief boy would be in bed with fever. This meant the tired rider must carry the *mochila* another fifty or even another hundred miles, stopping only to change horses and drink a bit of water.

Riders leaving St. Joseph often shouted news items to every station they passed. Like paperboys on street corners, they cried the headlines all the way to Sacramento:

"President Buchanan's Farewell Address to Congress!"

"Texas Leaves the Union!"

"Kansas Gets Its Statehood!"

"Congress Makes a Territory for Colorado!"

" . . . Nevada!"

" . . . Dakota!"

Then spring came and with it the event that sparked the quickest run ever — seven days, seventeen hours. Every boy and horse was pushed to go as fast as possible, so fast that two mustangs were galloped to death. Riders raced in pairs for safety, shouting together the word from Washington City: "Lincoln's Inaugural Address!"

Less than two weeks after Abraham Lincoln was sworn in as the sixteenth president of the United States, his speech was printed in San Francisco newspapers. No longer would Americans joke that news had already been forgotten in the east by the time folks in the west heard it.

One month later, when Jimmy learned that Confederates had fired on Fort Sumter in South Carolina, he had a bad feeling. He knew it meant civil war.

No one in the dusty way stations could foresee that this fighting between Northern and Southern states would last four long, terrible years. No one realized that hundreds of thousands would die.

After Jimmy shouted this story on a night run all the way to Roberts Creek Station, he returned to Ruby Valley the next morning in time for breakfast. Smoke wisping from the chimney brought the good smell of bacon frying and griddle cakes. He was famished. He couldn't wait to eat and to talk politics with Milo or whoever else was at the table.

But when he entered the cabin his heart sank. His friends Will and Nick Cone were rolling up their gear. Their boots were clean and they wore bright red bandanas with shirts that Mr. Tagg had washed and mended for them. Their young faces were eager.

"Jim!" they cried, happy to see him.

But Jimmy didn't smile. He looked at Milo, then back at his friends. "What're you fellas doing? Why are you packing?"

"We're going to war!" Nick announced. "Jimmy, we're going to be soldiers, real soldiers. The Confederates need us."

Jimmy's shoulders dropped. "Why do you want to go to war? Why?" He squeezed his hands into fists, trying to think of words to discourage them. The memory of Washakie's war with the Crow was still a horrible scar inside him. Men died in wars. They were mutilated or crippled or blinded. Mothers would lose sons and brothers; they would lose husbands. How could Jimmy explain?

"We'll be heroes, Jim."

"*Heroes?*" Jimmy said, almost with a laugh. "You already are heroes, why do you wanna be heroes twice? You're riders for the Pony Express, like me and Pen, remember? We joined up together; we promised we'd stay together." He gestured to Milo as if to say, *Can't you stop them?*, but Milo and Mr. Tagg remained silent. Their eyes were sad.

A clatter from the approaching stage interrupted Jimmy. Before he could protest, the two excited brothers hurried out into the brisk April morning. While a fresh team was harnessed to the coach, Nick and Will tossed their bundles into the rear boot. They tried to console Jimmy.

"We'll be back to Salt Lake before you know it," said Will. "We got kin in Georgia so we'll be all right. Don't frown so, Jim, it'll go fast."

Slowly Jimmy took Will's hand, then Nick's. He wanted to embrace them both, but hesitated when he noticed passengers watching. Among them were three young riders, spiffed up and smiling like boys headed for war. Sam Melvin, Johnny Fry, and another boy he didn't know had quit the Pony and were going east to join the army. Jimmy wondered if they were breaking their contracts.

The dusty red coach pulled out. Arms waving out each side made it look like a strange creature scurrying away. Clouds of powdery white alkali rose from the trail as it sped on. Jimmy's heart was heavy. He would miss his friends and he would worry about them.

He wandered beyond the corral out into the sandy brush. After many minutes Mr. Tagg came looking for him, wiping his calloused hands on his apron.

"Come on in now, son," he said gently. "I know how you feel . . . I wish they weren't going myself. Milo and I each lost a brother at the Alamo in '36. That battle was terrible for so many families. Alls we can do, Jim, is ask the Lord to watch over Nick and Willie. That's all we can do."

18

AN OLD FRIEND

As the snow began to melt, wagons with families resumed their westward journeys. When Jimmy's bunk was needed for elderly or ill travelers, he and Pen slept outdoors. Near the corral they made a wide bed of hay three feet high. There they slept burrowed down out of the wind, wrapped in wool blankets, stars overhead.

Early one morning, when the eastern sky began to pale, Jimmy woke suddenly. For a moment he lay there, frightened, his heart racing. He listened.

Pen slept next to him, a light snore ruffling from his open mouth. Slowly Jimmy started to sit up, but as he did, something held his right arm down. When he saw the arrow, he fell back with a groan.

"Pen," he whispered, kicking his friend's foot. "Wake up, *get up*. I've been shot."

Another kick and Pen bolted upright. His curly blond hair was full of straw. Sleepily he bent over Jimmy, who was still moaning. His eyes strained in the darkness to see the wound, but when Pen touched the arrow, he realized it had only pierced the wide sleeve of Jimmy's shirt. It had plunged into the straw, missing his arm by inches.

Seeing an opportunity to play a trick, Pen shook his head, pretending to be sad. "They got you good this time, Jimmy. Mr. Tagg's gonna have to amputate. I'll fetch his hacksaw . . ."

"Wait, don't leave me!" cried Jimmy, but when he heard Pen snort with laughter, he took a better look at his arm. Secretly he hoped there would be blood or some kind of wound, even a scratch would do. But the only damage was that his sleeve tore when he yanked out the arrow. He gave Pen a playful shove.

"Quit it, we coulda both been scal — "

"You shoulda seen your face, Jim, you shoulda seen it. Like this," and Pen raised his eyebrows in mock horror, again collapsing in laughter.

Jimmy was embarrassed. He also was a little disappointed their haystack wasn't riddled with arrows, to prove they'd almost been killed. It would have made a splendid story to scare Lillian Zimmerman.

The gray dawn was cold. Jimmy settled deeper into the straw where it was warm. He studied the arrow. The shaft was smooth cherry wood, about eighteen inches long, and the tip was metal, not stone. This meant the tribe had been trading with white men for some time.

The feathers on the end were bluish, from the wings of a mountain bluebird. Jimmy felt a tingle of recognition. These past months on the desert, he had not seen one mountain bluebird. But he had seen them years ago, further north, in the land of the Shoshoni and Bannocks.

Jimmy looked closer. In the growing light he could see markings below the feathers. Slowly he rolled the arrow between his fingers. There were tiny scratches in the shape of *nampa*, a moccasin.

A wild joy rose inside Jimmy. He jumped to his feet and turned toward the cottonwoods that surrounded the oasis. In the shadows he thought he saw a horseman, watching. Jimmy raised the arrow over his head. In response, a cry came from the trees, the cry of a bluebird taking flight.

Jimmy's eyes filled. Nampa had found him. He was in the woods and he wanted Jimmy to follow.

19

A MESSAGE FOR JIMMY

Jimmy quickly shook out his boots in case of scorpions, then slipped them onto his bare feet.

"I'll be back," he called to Pen as he began running along the narrow trail. A black-tailed jackrabbit bounded out of the brush as he reached the oasis. Jimmy could smell Nampa before he saw him, a rich musky smell that reminded him of deerskin shirts, bear grease, and the smoky fires inside tipis.

"Dawii," came the familiar voice as Nampa slid off his horse and stepped into the clearing. For a moment they studied each other, then they rushed forward with a handshake that became a crushing embrace, the embrace of old friends.

Nampa laughed. "Scared you good, didn't I, Dawii?"

"Naw. I knew it was you all along."

Jimmy was surprised how easily he answered in Shoshoni, as if only yesterday he had left the tribe. He was more surprised though, that the Nampa who now stood before him was a young man. He wore buckskin leggings, fringed on the sides, and moccasins with a double row of blue beads across the toe. His bare chest was broader and his arms more muscular.

A thick scar ran from Nampa's left elbow up to his neck. Jimmy knew this wound was recent because it was shiny pink, and he wondered if Nampa had been hurt in battle.

His braids hung to his waist, the ends wrapped in strips of red cloth. His pompadour was brushed up high from his forehead with grease. A lock of hair by each ear was adorned with beads and tin rings. Nampa was a handsome fellow.

While they looked at each other with silent admiration, Jimmy felt a thrill. Nearly five years ago they had parted as fourteen-year-old boys. *Now Nampa and I are men*, he thought.

With a gesture from Nampa they sat down. A breeze stirred the leaves of the cottonwoods, a whisper in the otherwise still air. In the east, the orange tip of the sun rose above the horizon with a burst of light. The day had begun. Finally Nampa spoke.

"Old Mother is ill," he said. "She has lost her

sight and her breath is weak. She grieves for her *tybo* son who has not returned.''

Jimmy's mouth went dry. He looked at Nampa with eyes that asked, *How much longer will she live?*

Nampa's high cheekbones made his face appear strong; gone was the roundness of boyhood. After several long moments he answered, ''One, maybe two moons.''

Jimmy turned away. He was heartsick and at the same time furious with himself. *Why hadn't he gone back to his Shoshoni family sooner?* If he hadn't been so busy being a hero he might already be sitting with Old Mother in her tipi, helping to keep her fire warm. He could be carrying water for her in the little brass bucket she loved so much.

''Nampa, old friend, tell her I am coming. I will leave in three sleeps.'' Jimmy stood. He needed to tell Milo and Mr. Tagg, for his year contract was nearly up anyway. Three days would be long enough for them to find a rider to replace him. It would be enough time to rest his horse, to prepare for the long journey north.

Something else. The moment Jimmy saw Nampa, every doubt he'd ever had, vanished. He would return to the Shoshoni. More than anything in the world, he wanted to return.

20

THIEVES IN THE NIGHT

When Jimmy rode back from Roberts Creek the next evening, Milo hurried him inside and pressed a rifle into his arms.

"Paiutes, Jim. They're camped at Ruby Lake."

Jimmy was tired and hungry. He did not want there to be any fighting. "Maybe they're just hunting," he said, taking a seat at the table.

"Well, that would be all right by me, but these fellas are painted for war."

The sound of a horse squealing interrupted them, then there was the rumble of galloping hooves.

"The ponies!" Jimmy cried. He flung open the door and raced out into the darkness, cocking the rifle as he ran. He fired two warning shots, then tossed the gun to Milo. "Cover me!"

Jimmy ran. He could see the dim outline of the corral, the moving shapes of men and mustangs leaping over a broken rail. It would be impossible to stop them, he knew this, but he had to try. Without horses, the mail would be delayed. Without a horse, Jimmy wouldn't be able to follow Nampa in two days as he had planned.

When he stumbled, he thought at first he'd bumped his head on a post. The pain brought him to his knees. He reached up to touch where it hurt, above his right eye, but there was something there — a stick. Then the ground met his back and he found himself staring up into the blurred face of Milo. Jimmy opened his mouth to speak, but no words came.

"Stay put, Jimmy, stay right there, don't move." Then under his breath Milo said, "Lord in heaven, we need your help."

Jimmy was aware of being carried into the cabin, of voices leaning over him. Only when he heard a snap, followed by a searing pain, did he realize Milo was trying to pull an arrow out of his skull. Again Jimmy's hand moved up, to feel the wound, as if by doing so it would help the sting go away.

But Mr. Tagg tied his arms to the bed, then his legs. He whispered in Jimmy's ear, "I'm so sorry to do this to you, son, but we need you to stop kicking. Milo's got to get that arrowhead out before it poisons you."

As Jimmy drifted into unconsciousness he felt as if he were still running, trying to catch his horse. He wanted to call for Nampa. *"Tell Old Mother I'm coming,''* he tried to yell. But he lacked the strength, and his voice was no louder than a whisper.

A distraught Pen Hailey was now at Jimmy's side, kneeling on the cold dirt floor. His hands were folded in prayer and as he looked heavenward, tears ran down his cheeks.

"Lord, don't let Jimmy die. Please."

Twenty minutes after midnight Billy Cody rode in from Deep Creek. When Mr. Tagg met him out by the empty corral, he gave him the bad news. Billy led his horse to water, then hurried into the stationhouse. He bent over his injured friend and, after getting a good look, turned wide-eyed to the others.

"Is he dead?" he asked.

"Not yet."

"He needs help. I'll fetch Doc Miller at Thorny Crik. Hang on, Spoon, hang on!" Billy drank a quick cup of water, then dashed out into the starry night.

His horse responded so swiftly that, by the time Mr. Tagg waved good-bye, they had become a small dark shape in the distance.

21

A MARRIAGE PROPOSAL

Jimmy didn't regain consciousness for six days. On the seventh morning his eyes opened. He tried to sit up, but his head throbbed as if a stone were bouncing inside his skull. A thick bandage prevented him from touching the wound.

When Milo saw Jimmy looking around, he jumped up from his stool. "Praise God," he cried. "The doc said you were a goner, but we refused to believe him. Jimmy, we've all been prayin' round the clock. Mr. Tagg," he yelled out the doorway, "Mr. Tagg, hurry. Jimmy's awake!"

By late afternoon Jimmy had managed to take a few steps by leaning against the bed rails. Though his left arm hung limp at his side and his left leg dragged, a smile was on his face. He didn't remember being shot, but he did remember Nampa's visit.

"Milo," he said slowly, "get my horse. I'm ready to leave."

It was evident to Milo that Jimmy wouldn't be able to walk on his own, let alone ride a horse several hundred miles north, but he did not want to discourage him. "Well, son, I guess you are ready," he said cheerfully. He offered Jimmy his elbow and helped him shuffle outside. Eight new horses were in the corral. The charred remains of one of the sheds was the only evidence that Ruby Valley Station had been attacked by Paiutes.

Jimmy stopped by the watering trough. Though the sun was low in the sky, its brightness hurt his eyes and made him so dizzy he began to weave. Milo caught him as he fell, then, in his strong arms, carried Jimmy back to his bunk.

"Well," Jimmy said as Milo gently tucked a pillow under his head. "Maybe I won't leave just yet. Maybe I'll have a bite of supper first."

"Now that's a right good idea, son. Mr. Tagg is making your favorite stew and we would all be mighty honored to have you at our table tonight."

Jimmy slept for seven more days and nights, waking only long enough to sip soup and be helped outside to relieve himself. Riders came and went, stagecoaches, too. Letters for Jimmy arrived in the *mochila*'s way pocket, the front right pouch that carried personal mail for each way station. Each stationmaster had a key to its little brass padlock.

When Lillian Zimmerman's perfumed envelope arrived, everyone in the room hovered near Jimmy, hoping he would read it aloud. It wasn't often that a girl would write one of the boys. Her letter — which had cost five dollars in postage — had been written on one sheet of tissue paper, both sides, in print so small Mr. Tagg had to put on his spectacles to help. Lillian's words were crowded into every possible space, sideways in margins, then upside down between lines. Mr. Tagg turned the letter here and there, squinting as if decoding a map. Finally he cleared his throat. " '*Dear Jimmy,*' " he began.

" '*We are all most horribly sorry about your mishap with the Indians and hope you'll soon come home to meet your new baby brother. His name is John. He is as fat as a little potato and he looks just like Thomas. Your mother is busy.*

" '*Your sisters Clara and Molly married Ezra Smith on the twenty-first and twenty-eighth of March respectively. I should think they are happy, even though Mr. Smith already has two other wives under the same roof. I personally plan not to share a husband's affections, and I would like to know if this is all right with you, Jimmy . . .*' " At this, Mr. Tagg stopped. His bushy white eyebrows raised in surprise.

"Why, Jim," he said, "if you'll forgive my editorial comment here, I do believe Miss Lillian is proposing marriage." He looked at the faces around him for confirmation.

Milo, who was on his stool nursing a mug of coffee, nodded slowly. "Yes, sir, I do believe that is what the young lady is trying to convey."

All eyes turned to Jimmy. He was sitting up in his bunk. Color had returned to his cheeks and the wound above his eye was a healthy pink. He didn't know what to make of Lillian's letter, except that he was pleased to hear his mother was well and that he had a new baby brother.

This made him think about his dear old Shoshone mother. How he missed her. She had been so kind and gentle to Jimmy. She had taught him so much. It wasn't fair that she was near death.

Now something else occurred to him. Jimmy had been so concerned about Old Mother's poor health that he'd forgotten to ask Nampa about Nahanee. He realized with a sudden race of his heart that she, too, would be five years older. She would be past the age when many Shoshoni girls married.

Nahanee. He must see her again. While his friends watched with concern, Jimmy eased himself off his bunk and braced himself against the table.

His throat was so tight, he swallowed hard to keep the lump down. "Can someone please help me get on my horse? I have to go north."

22

JIMMY'S SMALL VISITOR

Jimmy draped his arms over the corral gate and watched Mr. Tagg unsaddle the horses. It had been wonderful to ride again even though the bouncing at first made his head pound. But Milo had been firm: Jimmy was not ready to take on such a long journey alone; he would need to rest several more weeks.

Those stern words had filled Jimmy with despair. *Several more weeks.* By now Nampa would have returned to the Shoshoni camps and told Old Mother that Dawii was coming in three sleeps. She would be waiting for him, listening to every footstep that passed her tipi. Jimmy couldn't stand the thought of her dying. And worst of all, that she might die thinking he had broken a promise.

Also, there was Nahanee. Jimmy wasn't sure what he expected or wanted from the beautiful girl who had been his friend. All he knew was he wanted to be with her.

Someone was whistling "Yankee Doodle." Jimmy turned to see Pen boost himself onto the gate. His face was beaming. "Jim, you can leave in three days instead of three weeks and I know how!"

Jimmy looked up at his friend. There were bits of straw and leaves in the curly hair that Pen had trouble remembering to comb. His brown eyes were merry.

"What're you talking about?" Jimmy asked him, cautious.

"Milo just told me two more riders are being assigned to Ruby Valley on account of Billy Cody's hurt foot and one just for good measure. Think, Jim."

Jimmy gazed at a cloud for a moment, trying to understand. Finally he broke into a smile.

"Three days means a full moon. Are you coming with me, Pen?"

"If you'll let me."

"Will I!"

On a cool morning in May, a few days before Jimmy's nineteenth birthday, he and Pen gathered their gear. They planned to leave after the noon meal. For the first time in a year, Jimmy took out his eagle feather and tied it to the brim of his hat. Shoshoni honored the eagle as a symbol of strength and protection, and now that he was keeping his promise, Jimmy felt worthy to wear it.

From outside came Mr. Tagg's voice, announcing a visitor. Soon a wagon drawn by two mules pulled up in front of the cabin. When Mrs. Roberts swept down from the driver's seat, she pushed her sunbonnet back so it hung behind her. A large basket covered with gingham was on her left arm.

"Jimmy Spoon," she called. "You're not leaving without saying good-bye. We came fast as we could. Howdy, Milo, Mr. Tagg." She stepped into the dusky cabin, put the basket on the table, and pulled off the cloth. It was full of muffins as round and big as a man's fist.

When Jimmy stood up to greet her, he saw a small face peek around her skirt. "Ingabumbee!" he cried. "Come here, come to Jimmy."

The little boy toddled forward, one chubby hand still clinging to Mrs. Roberts's skirt. His red hair was fluffy, his cheeks rosy plump. He wore a long-sleeved gingham smock that almost covered his tiny bare feet. When Jimmy swooped him up, his wet diaper soaked the front of Jimmy's shirt.

"I am glad to see you, 'Bumbee, and I'm going to tell Old Mother all about you." Jimmy didn't complain about the diaper or mention that he had long ago hoped Ingabumbee could ride north with him. It mattered more to Jimmy that the child was happy with the Robertses. So far no relatives had come forward.

"My Lucy's with Tom and the fellas," said Mrs. Roberts. "Both her and 'Bumbee started walkin' a couple weeks ago and they are into everything, messy as two chipmunks. We can't stay. As it is, we'll have to camp at Diamond Springs again. I sure am gonna miss you, Jim." She crushed him to her with a hug stronger than Milo's. Jimmy would always remember how good Mrs. Roberts smelled, of fresh sunshine and sweat.

At one o'clock that afternoon Jimmy and Pen rode out of Ruby Valley. Farewells were quick. Milo had helped Jimmy into the stirrups, then from inside his shirt he took out the small Bible Jimmy had left on the hearth.

"You forgot to pack this, son."

"Didn't forget," Jimmy said. "I just don't need it. There's never time to read anyhow."

Milo smiled up at Jimmy, then patted him affectionately on the arm. "Well now, Jim, that's where I disagree with you." He tucked the Scriptures into Jimmy's saddlebag, slapped the horse's rump, then lifted his arm in a farewell wave as the animals broke into a gallop.

Milo and Mr. Tagg gave each other a sad smile, then they watched the northward trail. Soft white dust followed the boys long after they were out of sight.

23

THE HIDEOUT

Jimmy and Pen reached the northern end of the Ruby Mountain Range an hour before sunset. Shadowy canyons met the foothills, which were bushy with juniper and sage. Beyond was the desert, purple and brown in the waning light. They were far from the Overland Trail.

While the horses drank from a wide, shallow stream, Jimmy gathered twigs and leaves for the fire. He opened up a small leather pouch that had been smoked in beef fat to make it waterproof. Inside were the matches Mr. Tagg had made for them, short pieces of waxed cord dipped in sulphur. When rubbed against a rough stone, the tip ignited. It had the horrible smell of rotten eggs, but its blue flame quickly blazed through the kindling.

Jimmy was glad Pen was with him — for the companionship and so he could hunt the small game they would need for food. Jimmy's head ached so much at the end of a day he just wanted to lie down and sleep. Milo had been right. He was not well enough to travel alone.

Suddenly Pen appeared, running through the brush, the rifle swinging at his side. He was gesturing frantically and not until he reached Jimmy did he speak.

"Quick, Jimmy," he said, kicking dirt onto the flames, "put out the fire."

Jimmy hurriedly scooped sand into the pit. "Why? What is it?" he asked.

But Pen only motioned with his head. Together they untethered their horses and led them to a stand of cottonwoods on the other side of the stream. The bedrolls and gear were still tied to the saddles.

"Jimmy," he said in a low voice, "I heard men below the ridge there, drunken men. They were talking about a *murder*. Their horses are corraled in that box canyon we passed. What should we do?"

Jimmy stubbed at the ground with the toe of his boot. His head hurt and he was hungry. Soon it would be dark and they would need to eat. But the idea of spying on outlaws appealed to him more.

"Let's go see," Jimmy whispered.

With a nod, Pen slung the rifle over his shoulder. He led them into the stream where the sound of water would muffle their running. They followed it up to the south fork where white water flowed too swiftly for them to wade. Trailing its narrow beach they soon came to a fallen log that lay across the river, inches above the rapids. It was slippery with moss. With spray misting their arms and legs, the boys carefully crept along its trunk, through its tangle of roots, then onto shore.

Pen pointed to a thicket beyond the trees. When they reached it, they flattened themselves, face-down in a spongy bed of pine needles. Jimmy's feet squished uncomfortably in his boots as he crawled with Pen toward a ledge. From their bellies they looked below.

Eight men lounged around a campfire, all rough-looking characters, laughing loudly. A brown jug rolled in the dirt on its side, first kicked by one muddy boot, then another. Its missing cork indicated to Jimmy that whatever liquid had been in-side, was no longer.

His eyes widened when he noticed the dapper gentleman off to the side. The man looked familiar. He was cleaning a gun and laughing along with the others. When he turned slightly, revealing a handsome profile, Jimmy knew who it was.

Jack Slade.

So Milo and Mr. Tagg had been right. Jack Slade wasn't to be trusted. Maybe he *had* killed twenty-two people. Jimmy strained to see if there were any grisly mementos lying about, but saw only sacks of U.S. Mail and an assortment of luggage and small chests.

And he was in with the Rex Dooley gang! Jimmy began crawling backward, away from the ledge, pulling at Pen's soggy jeans so he would do the same. Another time, another day, Jimmy would have attempted a daring rescue of the mail. He would have stampeded their horses. He would have rounded up a posse to hunt down the thieves. A little danger would be exciting.

But today Jimmy wanted no trouble. He was wearing his eagle feather. Old Mother was waiting for him and he was not going to break a promise.

Moments before sunset, the boys made it back to the grove of cottonwoods. Without needing to speak, they pulled themselves into their saddles and rode out. A full moon was climbing skyward and, like a trusted old friend, it would help the boys see their way to safety.

24

BUFFALO

In the days that followed, the boys rode north along the outskirts of the lush Cache Valley in Utah Territory. Jimmy wanted to avoid the Mormon settlements. He did not want anyone to interrupt his journey with questions or offers of hospitality.

When they came to a rise and saw in the distance a shimmery thread of water, Jimmy became excited. This was *Piupa*, the Snake River, where he had first fished and swum with his Indian family. He and Pen had reached the Territory that Congress would soon name Idaho.

"There's Fort Hall," he said, pointing to the stockades in the grassy bottomland. Shoshoni traded here, which meant Jimmy might see old friends. Because the fort was on the Oregon Trail

96

it would also be bustling with travelers who stopped to rest and repair wagons. But as the boys came closer, they realized there was no smoke rising from the five chimneys and only a tattered rag dangled from the flagpole. The post was abandoned.

They rode through the empty yard to a bluff. Looking down, they found a steep trail to the river. While their horses drank, Jimmy and Pen took off their boots and trousers, unbuttoned their shirts, then raced each other in. The cold water felt good. Jimmy rolled onto his back and, as he did, he felt something brush his arm. A large speckled trout quickly twitched away from him, then swam to the middle of the current. This gave Jimmy an idea.

"Pen," he said in a quiet voice, "better build us a fire because I intend to catch us some dinner."

Jimmy let himself drift out to deeper water, facedown, his legs and arms floating like driftwood. Ever so slowly he turned his head to the side to take a breath. The water was crystal clear and he could see the trout's rainbowed tail finning back and forth.

Before the fish could blink, Jimmy's hand had glided under its belly, his fingers hooked the gills, and in one swift movement he tossed it to the bank. It landed flopping by Pen's muddy feet. Pen was so startled he dropped his shirt in the sand.

"Lordy Jim, I'm glad as heck you weren't catchin' us a bear for dinner."

* * *

For two days the boys continued north along *Piupa*, stopping often to water the horses and to let Jimmy rest under a shady tree. Though his wound had healed, he was bothered by headaches.

When the river turned east, Jimmy's heart quickened. He had camped here with Washakie. It was from that rock he had launched himself into a beautiful dive because Nahanee was watching and Jimmy had wanted to show off. Instead, he had landed such a slap on his belly, even now he cringed to remember his embarrassment.

The Teton Valley spread before them, gray-blue with sage and, in the far distance, the snowy western peaks of the Tetons. The beauty filled Jimmy with happiness. How wonderful those days were, when he was Dawii, Young Brother to the chief. The land was still lovely and it was alive. Sage grouse fluttered among the brush, and a family of pronghorn antelope scattered away from the trail, leaping as they ran. Overhead came the cry of a red-tailed hawk. Wind moved clouds across the sky as if pulling cotton; it stirred the tall grass.

Along the riverbank walked three big black birds, twice as large as crows. They looked like bullies, hunched over and serious, as they searched for seeds and bugs. Jimmy laughed out loud, pointing to them.

"You watch, Pen, soon those ravens will find a dead fish that floats ashore. Indians call them *The bird that never goes hungry*. They'll eat me and you if we sit still long enough. Come on!"

They rode to the top of a grassy knoll, then gal-

Buffalo

loped downhill for the fun of it. In the shade of an aspen they saw a light brown buffalo calf. Its mother was nearby, grazing on wheat grass. Her coat was dark brown with tufts of shedding fur.

"*Bojono,*" Jimmy whispered, remembering when Old Mother had taught him the word. *Buffalo.* Shoshoni followed the herds and lived well because of them. This meant his Indian family was closer than he'd realized. He wanted to hurry.

With each mile, more and more *bojono* dotted the landscape. Some would lift their huge furry heads to watch the two strangers on horseback. The boys rode for another hour, finally splashing through a shallow stream as they reached the crest of a hill. In the valley below was a sight that made Jimmy's heart swell with emotion.

Dozens of cone-shaped tipis were clustered near the river. Its sandy beach was noisy with children playing. Women worked over stretched-out hides and there was smoke from cooking fires. Men gathered in circles, possibly hunters and elders. A drumbeat came on the wind. On the other side of the river, a herd of spotted ponies moved among the grass.

Jimmy tried to take everything in. There was something so beautiful, something so deeply familiar, he knew this was a Shoshoni camp. But for a moment he felt sick. What if he was too late to see Old Mother alive? Would Nahanee be here? What about Nampa and Ga-mu, Poog and the others? Would they be angry he'd been away so long?

At the sight of so many Indians, Pen began to

shake. He touched Jimmy's sleeve. "We're out-numbered, Jim. Maybe I should turn back, maybe this wasn't such a good idea me comin' with you. Maybe they'll wanna scalp a white boy like me."

Jimmy smiled at his friend. Without explaining, he picked up the reins and clicked his tongue. His horse headed downhill, and in a dignified trot carried Jimmy toward the village.

25

WASHAKIE

A pack of barking dogs swarmed out to the meadow to meet Pen and Jimmy. This made Jimmy laugh. He remembered fondly how there were always dogs around camp; some were pets, but most were strays who made a lot of noise and dust when visitors came.

Three young boys on pintos galloped out, their braids flying and their small bare chests puffed up as if they were warriors. *"Yes, it is Dawii,"* one shouted as they circled the pair, then formed ranks. Proudly they escorted the newcomers into camp. Now Jimmy was certain his family was here; even these boys expected him.

As they crossed the meadow toward the tipis, Jimmy's heart beat fast. He was thrilled to see so many familiar faces in the crowd gathering around them. Children raced each other between the lodges to be first to get a good look. Someone called Jimmy's name, then someone else. An older woman he didn't recognize walked alongside his horse with her hand on his knee. She smiled up at him.

Pen, however, had never met an Indian, and now there were hundreds, all staring and wondering about him. He was so nervous, color had drained from his face. His stomach churned as if it might empty itself on the spot.

"Jimmy," he said. "I'm not feeling s'good." Even though Pen's words were not Shoshoni, the old woman seemed to understand. She came to his side and touched his hand. He let her help him from his saddle.

As several women guided Pen to a shady tree, Jimmy saw movement in the crowd to his right. He knew immediately that the tall man stepping out was Washakie. His war bonnet of eagle feathers looked like a high white crown, and his hair hung loose over his shoulders. He wore a shirt of blue cotton with a buckskin vest, beaded down the front.

"Dawii . . ." he said, motioning for someone to take Jimmy's horse. But the chief was too overcome with emotion to continue. His arms enfolded Jimmy with the affection he reserved for his family.

They walked along the river. It was late afternoon and sunlight glimmered off the water where tiny flies and mosquitos hovered. A fish broke the surface to feed, then with a small splash of its tail, swam down to the sandy bottom. For a long time Jimmy and Washakie sat cross-legged in the grass. Neither spoke.

After so many hours on horseback Jimmy's head hurt, but he didn't want to sleep, not yet. He drank in every familiar sight and sound. How good it was to hear children playing again, to hear the voices of women working together. Somewhere in the distance a man sang to a slow beat of a drum. Wood smoke drifted in the warm breeze, bringing with it the delicious aroma of roasting meat.

Jimmy glanced at Washakie's profile. He was still a handsome man. The deep scar under his left cheekbone was from an arrow long ago, a scar like Jimmy now had. Did he suffer from headaches, too? There was so much Jimmy wanted to ask his brother, so much he wanted to tell him.

For now though, they would enjoy each other's quiet company. Washakie would take him to see Old Mother when the time was right. Jimmy closed his eyes to savor the thought that had just come to him.

I am home. Finally, I am home.

26

A GENTLE SCOLDING

When the afternoon sun dipped below the tree-tops, long shadows spilled across the river. Washakie turned toward Jimmy.

"It is good you are here, Dawii. Our dear Old Mother asks for you and now I can tell her, *'Yes, Dawii has returned to us.'*"

He pointed to the wedge-shaped scar above Jimmy's eye and grinned. "But watch out, Old Mother will scold you for that."

After sunset Washakie took Jimmy to a tipi in the center of camp. He scratched on the outside. When a voice answered, he opened the flap, then ducked inside the oval doorway, motioning for Jimmy to follow.

It was dark except for a small fire in the center. Jimmy could see the shapes of three people sitting at the back of the lodge. One of them placed some dried buffalo droppings on the coals, then poked them until they blazed into a warm, smokeless fire. Yellow light swept up the sides of the tent.

Jimmy was overjoyed to see Old Mother. She sat between two of her daughters, staring toward him. Her unseeing eyes were milky white. She held out her arms for Jimmy, listening as he stepped around the fire to her. Tears of happiness rolled down her cheeks. She tried to talk, but her crying made her mouth shake and no words came.

"Old Mother," Jimmy said, coming to his knees to hug her. She was smaller than he'd remembered, but the tenderness in her embrace was the same. She held his face in her hands, as if to see him by touch. Her fingers felt his wet cheeks. She caressed his hair, his forehead, but when she discovered the smooth welt above his eye, she frowned.

"What has happened to my little son?"

"I met an Indian in the dark, Old Mother. He didn't like me."

"Aii! I knew there was trouble. In two more sleeps, if you had not come, Nampa and others were going to search for you. I knew you were hurt." She waved her hand as if to dismiss the thought, then leaned into her backrest. The excitement of the moment had exhausted her.

"Tell me about your family," she whispered.

"They know I've come to see you, Old Mother. I have a gift." Jimmy reached into his pocket and took out a blue silk scarf. Placing it in her hands he said, "My mother wants you to have this. She gave it to me when I left the Great Salt Lake City."

More tears filled the old woman's eyes, but she was smiling. Her fingers rubbed the fine silk. "Dawii," she said softly, "this is a happy day."

"Yes, Old Mother, it is."

27

JIMMY'S SEARCH

Two grandmothers set up a tipi for Jimmy and Pen on a raised bank near the river. They positioned it on the northeast side of a cottonwood tree so it would have sunshine in the morning, then shade in the afternoon when the day became hot.

The cover was made from moose hide and, when wrapped around the nine poles, looked like a short brown cone. The hem stopped two inches above ground, but a liner on the inside would keep out drafts and moisture.

Around the fire the women arranged two backrests, some cooking utensils, and a pile of kindling. Pen ran his hands over the thick dark fur of the buffalo robe that was to be his bed. He was fascinated how sunlight made the curved walls look golden and how, high overhead, the crisscross of poles formed a beautiful design. Blue sky showed through the opening.

"I declare, Jim, this beats that gloomy old cabin any day." Pen had recovered from his fright of the day before. The old woman named Singing Grass had cared for him as if he were her son; Pen-the-orphan was an orphan no more. On his feet was a new pair of moccasins, and he wore a long shirt made from soft deerskin. It was fringed at the knees and along the shoulders and sleeves.

"You look good," Jimmy told him. "Made you take a bath, didn't they?"

Pen laughed. His dark blond hair looked several shades lighter and gone were the bits of leaves and twigs that had nested in his curls. "Alls I could think of," he said, "was long ago when I was real, real little. A lady from the wagon train carried me into a river, then afterward dressed me in a big clean shirt of her husband's. It felt so good I wished she could have been my mother. That's what yesterday's bath made me remember."

Jimmy looked at his friend. "I'm glad you came with me, Pen. I wouldn't have made it all this way without you."

Every afternoon Old Mother's friends helped her walk to the riverbank where it was cool. Dappled sunlight filtered down through the cottonwoods where they sat listening to their grandchildren play. When Old Mother heard Jimmy approach, her face lifted with a smile.

"Dawii. I am ready to hear more from your book." She patted the ground next to her, inviting him to sit. Ever since she learned Jimmy had a Bible with words from *Bea Oppah*, the Great Spirit, she insisted he read and translate for her.

"Yes, Old Mother, I'll read. But first I must ask you something." Here Jimmy hesitated. He wished she understood English so he could talk without the others hearing. Instead, he leaned close and spoke in her ear.

"Old Mother," he said, "since I came eight suns ago, I have looked through camp and beyond. I have not seen Nahanee or her family."

Old Mother nodded. "Nor have I seen her." She laughed at her joke, then stopped herself. Dawii was speaking from his heart; this was not the time to tease.

"Many have gone to the river north of here," she offered, "to welcome back the Leaping Fish with a blessing ceremony. Washakie is there."

Jimmy knew Old Mother was talking about the chinook salmon and their annual return from the ocean. The ceremony was sacred, with hours of prayer and thanksgiving. Like the buffalo, salmon were respected and honored because year after year they sustained the people.

"Before the snows," Old Mother continued, "Nahanee was here. She and her mother made moccasins for me. We talked about the bear and we talked about you."

Jimmy's heart leapt. Nahanee hadn't forgotten

him after all. "What did she say about me?" he asked.

Old Mother listened to the river for several moments before answering. "There are many things on a young woman's heart when each moon passes."

What did Old Mother mean? Was Nahanee in love with someone? Jimmy was afraid to ask, because he was afraid of what the answer might be. He remembered something from long ago. It was the evening after he had rescued Nahanee from the grizzly bear. By the fire in Washakie's tipi her grateful parents promised him a gift: Their daughter Nahanee would one day be his bride.

But Jimmy had said no. *I do not want a wife.* Those words now haunted him.

"Old Mother," he said. "I am going to go north to welcome the Leaping Fish. When I return, you and I will have much to talk about."

"Yes, son, I know."

28

BIG FISH GIRL

The next day Pen and Jimmy saddled their horses and set out with three others: Mozo the elder, Nampa, and Ga-mu, old friends of Jimmy's. They rode north toward the river that white men would one day name the Salmon.

The timbered hills were lush from melting snow. Waterfalls could be heard, a high whisper in the clear air. Everywhere, Jimmy recognized land-marks. *I am home*, he wanted to shout.

The river twisted through canyons. Bighorn sheep blended into the hillsides so perfectly that only when they leapt from rock to rock could Jimmy see the animals. After two days of travel there was a wide pebbled beach and, in the middle of the river, a sandbar where four tipis were camped.

"We'll rest here," Mozo said. He dismounted carefully, as if his legs were stiff. His silver braids were wrapped halfway down with otter fur and there were two eagle feathers at his temple. Jimmy felt deep admiration for Mozo. He took the reins of his horse, then helped Ga-mu turn the others to pasture.

In the narrow part of the stream, a large boulder formed a bridge, making it easy to cross over to the island without getting moccasins wet. A woman with a cradleboard on her back greeted the travelers, then called to someone inside her lodge. Out stepped an attractive girl about Jimmy's age. She was quite round with a plump face, a familiar face.

It was Big Fish Girl and Jimmy was not glad to see her. Not only was she bossy, she weighed at least eighty pounds more than he did, which meant she could wrestle him down in a wink. Many times they had quarreled. Once he called her a bad name and she had shoved him into a marsh and snapped his hunting bow in half. Jimmy eventually decided to be nice to her. He knew it would be safer to wrestle a grizzly than to make Big Fish Girl mad again.

"Hello, Dawii," she smiled. "I see you found me." She turned away and began walking toward the far end of the campsite. Since Nampa and the others were talking, Jimmy followed Big Fish Girl. They sat down on the tip of the sandbar where the river flowed past them on both sides, as if they were in the bow of a canoe

She turned her brown eyes on him. "I've waited a long time for you," she said. Her boldness embarrassed Jimmy. He glanced back at the four tipis, hoping to see Nahanee or her mother.

After an awkward silence he finally spoke. "Mozo is taking us to the Blessing Ceremony. I want to see old friends."

Big Fish Girl's face darkened. "If you're looking for Nahanee, you are too late."

Jimmy glared at her. "What are you saying?" he asked. His heart was beating fast and he felt a tightness in his throat.

"I am saying that you are eight moons too late. Nahanee has a husband. She is big with child. But I, who waited patiently, am not married. My lodge is yours, Dawii. I will make you very warm when the snows come."

But Jimmy wasn't listening. He felt dizzy and suddenly his head hurt so much he wanted to lie down. If only he could sleep, he might have the courage to turn back.

This wasn't his home after all. He hated it here. He hated the smiling round face of Big Fish Girl.

29

THE NECKLACE

Pen noticed Jimmy with the horses. "Jim!" he called, running across the field. "Where're you going?"

Jimmy stroked the muscular neck of his pinto. His eyes were sad. "I'm going back," he said. "I'll wait with Old Mother until you and the others return, then we'll ride together to Salt Lake City."

"But why? Why are you leaving? I don't understand. Was that girl the one you're looking for, is she Nahanee?"

"*Her?* No. That's Big Fish Girl. She thinks she owns the world. Every time I see her I have bad dreams."

Pen threw his hands up in frustration. "You're leaving because of her? She's just a girl."

114

Jimmy closed his eyes and lay his head on the horse's silky mane. He was heartbroken that Nahanee had married. If only he'd realized she meant so much to him, he never would have stayed away so long.

Wanting to comfort him, Pen touched Jimmy's shoulder. He didn't know what to say.

"I should have come sooner," Jimmy said miserably.

A voice distracted them. They looked up to see Mozo walking slowly toward them. The elder's arm was raised as if to say *don't go*.

When Jimmy explained why he wanted to leave, Mozo was quiet. Finally he nodded as if he understood. "I cannot tell you what to do, Dawii. But I can tell you it is not good to hide when the heart is sad. Come to the Blessing Ceremony. You will learn there is much to be thankful for, even when you're unhappy. That is all I have to say."

Mozo walked back to the sandbar where there was smoke from two campfires. The good smell of fish roasting made Jimmy hungry. He thought about Old Mother and remembered how she once scolded him for disobeying Mozo.

Have you lived so long that you know more than your elders? is what she'd said.

Because Jimmy hadn't listened to Mozo, he ended up lost in the woods, alone. He did not want to make another mistake like that and he did not want to be like Mr. Lantern, a man who thought his way was the only way.

Jimmy looked at Pen and tried to smile. "I've changed my mind," he said. "Let's join the others."

The next day, they continued north. Jimmy counted nineteen tipis near the river. There were dogs and children and cooking fires; there were boys on ponies racing each other below a hillside. Some of them cantered over to escort the travelers into camp. Jimmy didn't feel the excitement he'd felt two weeks earlier. His heart was heavy thinking about Nahanee. He slid off his horse and handed the reins to a boy eager to help.

Pen was surrounded by children who'd never before seen such yellow hair or freckled skin. He was not nervous this time; instead he was friendly. Pen was enjoying his new status as Friend of Dawii, Son of Singing Grass.

A group of mothers and daughters watched Jimmy fondly. When he saw Nahanee among them his heart fell, but then it soared with happiness.

She stood in front of her lodge, her eyes cast down to show respect. She was more beautiful than Jimmy had remembered and when she lifted her head to smile at him he thought he would burst with joy.

Big Fish Girl had lied. Nahanee was not big with child. Her soft deerskin dress fell gracefully over her slim figure. Around her neck was the magnificent bear claw necklace Jimmy had given her five years ago.

Nahanee had waited for Dawii to return and she was wearing his necklace to say so.

30

THE BLESSING

Jimmy and Nahanee wandered along a creek where fragrant white flowers of the syringa bloomed. In the shady woods there were violets, blue and yellow, and ferns. As they talked, Jimmy was aware of the aroma of balsam and pine, and the pleasant twittering of birds. Never had he known a more beautiful day or a happier moment, but he did know this: He loved Nahanee with all his heart.

When they stopped by a small waterfall, he found himself gently pulling her to him. He breathed in the wonderful scent of her hair and skin. They glanced at each other, then laughed at their shyness. Jimmy wanted to kiss her, but he wasn't sure how to go about it.

"Nahanee," he said, holding her hands in his. He gazed at her lovely face and felt lost for words. "I . . . I . . . want to marry you, Nahanee."

She looked into his eyes. "I will be your woman, Dawii."

Jimmy let out a huge sigh of relief, then threw his head back in laughter. No longer shy, he swept her into a hug. With one hand under her head and an arm around her waist, he kissed her.

Nahanee was going to be his wife. Wild with joy, he kissed her again.

Later that afternoon Jimmy found Pen by the river with Mozo, who was showing him how to string a bow. There was something about Jimmy's manner that made them both stop and look at him.

"Big Fish Girl lied, didn't she?" asked Pen.

Jimmy laughed. "Yes." He picked up a small, flat stone and threw it low so that it skipped several times across the water. He picked up another stone. This one he rolled between his fingers, thinking.

"Nahanee and I will marry before the snows," he said. "Pen, I won't be returning to Salt Lake, at least not for a while."

Jimmy translated for his elder. A light breeze moved the ends of Mozo's gray hair, which hung loose down his back. He grinned. "You will be warmer than most of us, Dawii. This is good that you have come back to us."

"Yes, Mozo, I am glad to be home." In English, Jimmy said, "Pen, if you don't mind wintering here, I will ride back with you in the spring, then my family will be able to meet my wife. What we'll do then, I'm not sure."

Pen's eyes widened and he gave Jimmy's shoulder a hearty shake. "Count me in. I wouldn't miss that for anything."

Before dawn the next morning families began to gather in a clearing by the river, forming a semicircle. The air was cold. Some mothers had babies in cradleboards, others left their smaller children sleeping in the lodges.

The Blessing Ceremony began the moment the first rays of sunlight split through the trees. Washakie and Mozo stood near the fire where the fragrance of cedar and sweet sage rose with the smoke. They held fans made of eagle feathers, which they waved through the incense. A slow drumbeat marked time.

Jimmy and Nahanee walked with the others past the fire, praying silently, then sipping from a gourd of river water. Pen followed with his new friends, Nampa and Ga-mu. Mozo raised his arms to the sky and began to sing:

"*Bea Oppah*, grant the Leaping Fish a safe return . . . *Bea Oppah*, grant us peace . . ."

Jimmy looked at Nahanee. Sunlight lay on her cheek, her eyes were closed with reverence. How good she was. How he loved her.

As the hour passed, Jimmy began to feel a deep peace. Mozo was right, there was always something to be thankful for. He thought about his family in Salt Lake and about his friends Will and Nick Cone, Mr. Tagg and Milo, little Ingabumbee.

"*Bea Oppah*, take care of them all," Jimmy sang. "*Bea Oppah*, help me be a good husband." He took Nahanee's hand, then raised his face to the sun.

AFTERWORD

Jimmy Spoon and the Pony Express is a blend of history and fiction. For example, Billy (William F. "Buffalo Bill") Cody was one of the youngest riders at age fourteen, but his route was actually east of Utah.

Joseph Alfred ("Captain Jack") Slade rode between Fort Laramie and Horseshoe Station in Wyoming. He was one of the more notorious riders, a whiskey guzzler and desperado who boasted of twenty-six murders. Eventually he was hanged by vigilantes in Virginia City, Montana.

Twenty-three-year-old James Butler ("Wild Bill") Hickok was not a Pony Express rider, but he was a stable hand at the Rock Creek Station near the Kansas-Nebraska state line. It was there by the

Little Blue River that on the hot, dusty day of July 12, 1861, he killed several members of the Mc-Canles gang. Accounts vary, but one legend says that David McCanles enjoyed making fun of Hickok's protruding upper lip by calling him "Duck Bill." This teasing may or may not have led up to the murder. As a result, "Duck Bill" became "Wild Bill," a gunslinger and U.S. Marshal of Abilene, Kansas. It is said, however, that he spent much of his time at the poker table.

During the summer of 1861, brothers Samuel and Orion Clemens traveled by stagecoach from Missouri to Carson City, thrilling to the sight of a Pony Express rider. Because of the heat — and because there were no female passengers — they rode much of the way in their Skivvies. Orion became assistant to Governor James W. Nye of the newly formed Nevada Territory. For some time Sam was Orion's assistant, then he took a job reporting for the Virginia City *Territorial Enterprise*, writing under the name of Mark Twain. He describes these adventures and his meetings with Brigham Young and Jack Slade in *Roughing It*, published in 1872.

Historians disagree about the exact numbers and locations of Pony Express Stations in Nevada. A few stone foundations and crumbling adobe walls exist, but most remnants are gone. Exceptions are Fort Churchill, which is now a state monument, and the blacksmith shop at Friday's Station. Some of the original log cabin from Ruby Valley Station was moved and reconstructed; it is now displayed at the Northeastern Nevada Museum in Elko.

Alexander Majors did issue each boy a Holy Bible, believing their spiritual health was as important as their physical health. *Jimmy Spoon* is not the complete story of the Pony Express, nor does it begin to tell about the many heroes and colorful events. Some of the fine books listed in the bibliography do that.

GLOSSARY

[*Sho.*: Shoshoni, *Sp.*: Spanish]

alkali — salty, fine dirt found in deserts where a lake or pond has evaporated

Bea Oppah — [*Sho.*]; Great Father, Great Spirit, God

Bannock — "hair in backward motion," referring to men's pompadour, Idaho tribe

bojono — [*Sho.*]; buffalo

Conestoga — a covered wagon used by pioneers; named after Conestoga Valley, Pennsylvania, where the wagons were built

Confederates — soldiers from the league of Southern States that seceded from the United States in 1860–61 (Alabama, Arkansas, Florida, Georgia, Louisiana, Mississippi, North Carolina, South Carolina, Tennessee, Texas, and Virginia)

Dawii — [*Sho.*]; young brother

Ga-mu — [*Sho.*]; rabbit

Gosiute — "dust people," a Shoshoni-speaking tribe from the southwest area of Utah's Great Salt Lake and parts of Nevada

Ingabumbee — [*Sho.*]; red hair

mestengo — [*Sp.*]; wild (mustang horse)

124

Glossary

mochila — [*Sp.*]; knapsack (the leather rectangle with four mail pouches that fits over the pommel and cantle of the Pony Express rider's saddle; total weight was less than thirteen pounds, or one third of an ordinary western saddle)

Mozo — [*Sho.*]; whisker

Nampa — [*Sho.*]; moccasin

Paiute — "Ute of the water," Nevada tribe

Piupa — [*Sho.*]; Snake River

Skivvies — a man's short-sleeved undershirt/underwear

Tosa-ibi — [*Sho.*]; Soda Springs, Idaho

transcontinental telegraph — the coast-to-coast planting of telegraph poles that finally met in Salt Lake City, Utah, on October 24, 1861

tybo — [*Sho.*]; white person

Washakie — [*Sho.*]; rawhide rattle

BIBLIOGRAPHY

Bloss, Roy S. *Pony Express, The Great Gamble.* Berkeley, CA: Howell-North, 1959.

Bowman, John S., gen. ed. *The World Almanac of the American West.* New York: World Almanac, 1986.

Bradley, Glenn D. *The Story of the Pony Express.* Chicago: A. C. McClurg & Co., 1913.

Capps, Benjamin. *The Great Chiefs.* Alexandria, VA: Time-Life Books, 1975.

Chapman, Arthur. *The Pony Express.* New York: Putnam's, 1932.

Cody, William F. *The Life and Adventures of "Buffalo Bill," an Autobiography.* Clinton, MA: The Colonial Press, 1927.

Corporation of the President of The Church of Jesus Christ of Latter-day Saints. *The Beehive House.* Salt Lake City, UT: 1978.

Curran, Harold. *Fearful Crossing: The Central Overland Trail Through Nevada.* Las Vegas: Nevada Publishers, 1982.

Deseret News. Salt Lake City, UT: 1850–1860.

Grun, Bernard. *The Timetables of History.* New York: Simon & Schuster, 1982.

Jensen, Lee. *The Pony Express.* New York: Grosset & Dunlap, 1955.

Lennon, Nigey. *The Sagebrush Bohemian: Mark Twain in California.* New York: Paragon House, 1990.

Madsen, Brigham D. *The Shoshoni Frontier and the Bear River Massacre.* Salt Lake City: University of Utah Press, 1985.

Nevada Bureau of Land Management. *The Pony Express in Nevada.* Lake Tahoe, NV: 1976.

Nevin, David. *The Expressmen.* New York: Time-Life Books, 1974.

Patent, Dorothy Hinshaw; photographs by William Munoz. *Where the Wild Horses Roam.* New York: Clarion Books, 1989.

Perry, John, and Jane Greverus Perry. *The Sierra Club Guide to the Natural Areas of New Mexico, Arizona and Nevada.* San Francisco: Sierra Club Books, 1985.

Reinfeld, Fred. *Pony Express.* New York: Macmillan, 1966.

Robertson, James I., Jr. *Civil War! America Becomes One Nation.* New York: Knopf, 1992.

Root, Frank A. *The Overland Stage to California.* Topeka, KS: W.Y. Morgan, 1901.

Seymour, John. *The Forgotten Household Crafts.* New York: Knopf, 1987.

Sho-Ban News. Fort Hall, ID: 1987–1992.

Spencer, Clarissa Young, with Mabel Harmer. *Brigham Young At Home.* Salt Lake City: Schocken Books, 1982.

Stein, R. Conrad. *The Story of the Pony Express.* Chicago: Children's Press, 1981.

Stevenson, Augusta. *Buffalo Bill, Boy of the Plains.*

New York: Bobbs-Merrill, 1948.

Storer, Tracy I., and Robert L. Usinger. *Sierra Nevada Natural History*. Berkeley: University of California Press, 1963.

Twain, Mark. *Roughing It*. Hartford, CT: American Publishing Co., 1872; New York: New American Library, 1962.

Visscher, William Lightfoot. *The Pony Express*. Chicago: The Charles T. Powner Co., 1908, 1946.

Waldman, Carl; maps and illustrations by Molly Brown. *Atlas of the North American Indian*. New York: Facts on File Publications, 1985.

Wheeler, Sessions S. *The Nevada Desert*. Caldwell, ID: Caxton Printers, Ltd., 1989.

Williamson, Darcy, and Steven Shephard. *Salmon River Legends and Campfire Cuisine*. Bend, OR: Maverick Publications, 1988.

Wilson, Elijah Nicholas. *Among the Shoshones*. Medford, OR: Pine Cone Publishers, 1910.

ABOUT THE AUTHOR

Kristiana Gregory is a noted author of historical fiction for young readers. Her books have been nominated for numerous state awards, and her first novel, *Jenny of the Tetons*, won the 1989 Golden Kite Award for fiction. Her most recent novel, *Earthquake at Dawn*, was an ALA Best Book for Young Adults.

Ms. Gregory lives in California with her family.

Kids love Barbara Park's books so much, they've given them all these awards:

Georgia Children's Book Award

IRA-CBC Children's Choice

Maud Hart Lovelace Award (Minnesota)

Milner Award (Georgia)

OMAR Award (Indiana)

Tennessee Children's Choice Book Award

Texas Bluebonnet Award

Utah Children's Book Award

Young Hoosier Book Award (Indiana)

Bullseye Books™ by Barbara Park:

Almost Starring Skinnybones

Beanpole

Dear God, Help!!! Love, Earl

Don't Make Me Smile

The Kid in the Red Jacket

Maxie, Rosie, and Earl—Partners in Grime

My Mother Got Married (And Other Disasters)

Operation: Dump the Chump

Rosie Swanson: Fourth-Grade Geek for President

Skinnybones

Skinnybones

BARBARA PARK

BULLSEYE BOOKS • RANDOM HOUSE
NEW YORK

To Steven and David, for all your inspiration

Skinnybones

chapter one

MY CAT EATS KITTY FRITTERS BECAUSE...

I figure that if she *didn't* eat Kitty Fritters, she would probably be dead by now.

Kitty Fritters is the only cat food my mother will buy. She buys it because she says it's cheap. She says she doesn't care how it tastes, or what it's made out of. My mother is not the kind of person who believes that an animal is a member of the family. She is one of those people who thinks a cat is just a cat.

I have an aunt who thinks that her cat is a real person. Every time we go over there, she has her cat dressed up in this little sweater that says FOXY KITTY on the front.

This aunt of mine wouldn't be caught dead giving her cat Kitty Fritters. She says that Kitty Fritters taste like rubber. I'd hate to think that my aunt has actually tasted Kitty Fritters herself, but how else would she know? My mother says that my aunt is a very sick person.

Anyway, I think you should keep on making Kitty Fritters as long as there are people like my mother, who don't think cats mind eating rubber.

THE END

After I finished writing, I went to the closet and took the bag of Kitty Fritters off the bottom shelf. I turned to the back of the bag and read the rest of the directions. It said:

COMPLETE THIS SENTENCE:
MY CAT EATS KITTY FRITTERS BECAUSE . .
Then print your name and address on the entry
blank enclosed in this bag. Mail your entry to:

KITTY FRITTERS TV CONTEST
P. O. Box 2343
Philadelphia, Pennsylvania 19103

I dug down into the bag, trying to find the entry blank. I couldn't feel it anywhere. I tried again, reaching down into the other side of the bag. It wasn't there either. Finally I put the bag between my legs, and stuck both of my arms all the way down to the very bottom. I still couldn't find it!

Finally I got so frustrated, I dumped the entire ten-pound bag of cat food out onto the kitchen floor. I must have sifted through about a million little fritters before I finally found the entry blank. Carefully, I placed it on the kitchen counter and filled it out.

NAME: Alex Frankovitch
ADDRESS: 2567 Delaney Street
CITY: Phoenix   STATE: Arizona   ZIP: 85004

Just as I was finishing up, I heard the cat scratching at the door. I figured that she had probably smelled the disgusting odor of fritters all the way down the block.

"Go away!" I shouted. "You can't come in right now I'm busy!"

I just *had* to get the cat food mess cleaned up before my mother got home.

"Alex Frankovitch! You open this door!" shouted my cat. My cat? Oh no! Suddenly, I realized that it had been my *mother* scratching at the door.

I hurried to let her in.

"Why were you scratching at the door?" I asked when I opened it. It was a very stupid question. She was carrying two large bags of groceries.

"I wasn't scratching," she answered as she hustled by me. "I banged on it with my foot!"

After putting the groceries on the counter, my mother glanced down at the millions of little fritters scattered all over the floor. All things considered, I think she took it very well.

"Been fixing yourself a little snack, Alex?" she asked, sounding slightly annoyed.

I figured that there were two different ways of handling my problem. First of all, I could try to get my mother to laugh about the whole thing. If *that* failed, I would have to move on to Plan Two: Blame It on the Cat.

"Snack? What snack?" I asked, trying to sound very serious. "I haven't been fixing a snack."

"I *mean* all these Kitty Fritters, Alex," said my mother, even more annoyed than before.

"Kitty Fritters?" I asked, looking all around. "What Kitty Fritters?"

This was where she was supposed to start laughing. But unfortunately, she didn't.

"I'm waiting for an explanation, Alex," she said, folding her arms. Whenever my mother folds her arms, she means business. Quickly, I moved on to Plan Two.

"Oh . . . *those* Kitty Fritters!" I said, pointing at the floor. "Well, you're probably not going to believe this, but while you were gone I was sitting in the den watching TV—"

"Now, *that* I believe," interrupted my mother. "It seems that all you've been doing lately is watching that stupid TV."

"Listen, Mother," I said, "do you want to hear what happened, or not?"

"Okay, Alex," she said, "you may continue."

"Well, anyway," I said, "there I was watching TV, when all of a sudden, I heard this loud crash come from the kitchen. I ran in here just in time to see the cat running out the back door. That's when I looked down and saw this giant mess of fritters."

My mother just stared at me for a minute. Then she said, "Are you *positive* that's what happened, Alex?"

I couldn't believe it. My mother was actually going to believe that stupid story. Wow! For the very first time, I was really going to get away with something. Usually I *never* get away with *anything*!

"Positive, Mom," I replied. "Honest, that's exactly what happened. The cat must have tried to get something to eat and knocked the bag over."

My mother walked over and put her hand on my shoulder. "In that case, Alex," she said, "could you please do me a big favor?"

"Aw, come on, Mom!" I said, trying to sound upset. "You're not going to make me clean this whole mess up, are you? That's really not fair. I just told you I didn't do it!"

"No, Alex, that's *not* what I wanted," she said with a very strange grin on her face. "What I want you to do is to go and get the cat out of the car. I just brought her home from the vet's. I took her to get her shots."

Now, most people think that when you get caught in a giant lie like that you're doomed. But not me. I've always said, "A good liar never gives up without a fight."

"Boy, that really makes me mad!" I shouted.

"What makes you mad, Alex?" asked my mother. "Being caught in a stupid, ridiculous lie like that?"

"Lie? What lie? What are you talking about, Mom? No," I said, "the thing that makes me mad is that one of Fluffy's little friends would come in here, make a big mess, and then try to run away

8

and blame it on poor little Fluffy! Boy, when I find out which neighborhood cat did this, he's *really* going to be sorry."

Then I hurried outside and got Fluffy from the car. As I walked back into the house, I kept talking to the cat so that my mother wouldn't have a chance to say anything.

"Fluffy, you're not going to believe this, but one of your little buddies almost got you in very big trouble! If you ask me, I think it was probably Fritzi, from down the street. I've always thought that Fritzi was the sneaky type—"

"Alex . . . Alex!" shouted my mother, interrupting me.

"Yes, Mom?"

"Give up," she said.

"Give up?" I asked. "What do you mean, give up?"

"I mean, you're making a fool out of yourself, Alex," she said.

I paused for a minute and looked up. "Does this mean that you don't believe me?"

"Let me put it this way, Alex," my mother replied. "If you were Pinocchio, right now we'd have enough firewood to last the winter."

Then she handed me a broom and started out of the room.

"Don't look so glum," she said as she left. "If it

will make you feel any better, that was the most creative fib you've told in weeks."

I thought about it.

It didn't make me feel better.

As soon as she was gone, I started sweeping the Kitty Fritters back into the bag. Meanwhile, Fluffy had begun to eat every single fritter in sight.

I just couldn't seem to get the darned things back into the bag fast enough. Fluffy was really packing them in. Getting shots must give cats quite an appetite.

It took about ten minutes before I was finished cleaning up the floor. By that time, I could tell that Fluffy was getting pretty full. But she never stopped eating . . . not until the last Kitty Fritter was in the bag.

As I put the bag back on the bottom shelf, my mother came in to inspect the floor. The cat ran to greet her. My mother stared at her for a minute.

"Why does Fluffy look so puffy?" she asked.

"I guess it must be all those Kitty Fritters she ate while I was trying to get them cleaned up," I explained.

"Oh, Alex!" my mother cried. "Those things will swell up in her stomach and make her very sick! She's not supposed to have too many!"

10

My mother looked worried.

I would have been worried too, but just then Fluffy walked over to where I was standing and threw up on my shoe. It was the most disgusting thing that ever happened to me.

My mother started laughing.

"This is not funny!" I shouted. But my mother couldn't seem to stop. If you ask me, I think she was acting pretty childish.

After a couple of minutes, she walked over and picked up the cat. "Honestly, Fluffy," she said, "if you don't like Alex's shoes, all you have to do is *say* so." Then she started laughing all over again.

I think I probably would have felt a lot worse, but my mother was laughing so hard that she forgot to punish me for lying to her. Getting her to laugh always works. I just wish I could have done it without having Fluffy throw up on me.

chapter two

The first time that I can remember making people laugh was in kindergarten. Every morning, the teacher would ask if anyone had anything special for Show and Tell.

At first I was pretty shy. I would just sit there quietly at my desk and keep my mouth shut. But there were lots of kids who didn't.

There was this one kid named Peter Donnelly who sat in front of me. Every single day, when the teacher asked if anyone had anything for Show and Tell, dumb old Peter Donnelly would raise his hand.

Sometimes he brought in hobbies. Peter had the stupidest hobbies in the whole world. One of his hobbies was collecting different-colored fuzz. Weird, right?

One day he brought his fuzz collection to school. He kept it in a shoe box. When he passed it around, I felt stupid just looking at it.

Then, all of a sudden, I got this funny idea. Just as I was about to pass the box to the next person, I pretended that I was going to sneeze.

"AH . . . AH . . . AHCHOO!"

I sneezed right smack in the middle of Peter's fuzz collection. Fuzz balls went flying everywhere. The whole class began to laugh at once.

Peter panicked. He rushed over to my desk and began gathering up his fuzz collection and putting it back in his box. The teacher told me to help him, but I was laughing too hard to get out of my chair. I had to admit, making people laugh was a lot more fun than sitting quietly in my seat. I decided I would have to do it more often.

From then on, I began to use Show and Tell to tell the class funny things that had happened to me. When I ran out of true things to tell, I started making them up.

One time I told the class that my father was a raisin. I don't know what made me say such a silly thing. But it sure sounded funny.

The teacher made me sit down. She said that

there was a big difference between Show and Tell and Show and Fib. Personally, I don't think teachers like it when their students are funnier than they are. I ought to know. So far I've been funnier than every teacher I've ever had. And not one of them has liked me. My goal in life is to try and find a teacher who appreciates my sense of humor.

Last year I had a teacher named Miss Henderson. So far, out of all the teachers I've ever had, Miss Henderson is the one who disliked me the most.

I'm not really sure why. In the fifth grade, I was the funniest I've ever been. You'd think a teacher would like it when a student tries to brighten up the day with a little joke or two.

On the very first day of school, I knew Miss Henderson wasn't going to like me. She made everyone stand up next to their desk and introduce themselves to the class. Boy, do I hate that! You were supposed to tell your name, where you were born, and something about your family. Allison Martin started.

She said, "My name is Allison Martin. I was born right here in Phoenix, and I have two brothers."

Whoopee for you, I thought to myself.

Then, Brenda Ferguson stood up. "My name

14

is Brenda Ferguson. I was born in California, and I have a baby sister."

And you're also very dumb, I thought.

This had to be the most boring thing I had ever listened to in my life. After about six kids had spoken, I just couldn't stand it anymore. I raised my hand.

"Yes," said Miss Henderson. "You there, in the yellow shirt."

I looked down at my shirt. Yup. It was yellow all right. I stood up.

"Miss Henderson," I said, "this is getting kind of boring. Couldn't we try to tell something a little more interesting about ourselves?"

Miss Henderson thought about it for a minute and then gave me a little smile.

"Okay, then," she said finally. "Why don't you start us off? Tell us who you are and something interesting about yourself."

Wow! I thought to myself. Maybe for once, I've got a teacher who is going to appreciate me.

"Okay," I said. "My name is Alex Frankovitch. I was born in Phoenix, and my mother is a land turtle."

Miss Henderson didn't laugh. Instead she gave me a dirty look and motioned for me to sit down.

By this time, the whole class was roaring, and

Miss Henderson had to beat on her desk with a ruler. For a minute there, I actually started feeling a little sorry for her. But it didn't last long. As soon as she got the class under control, she continued with the same boring stuff we had been doing before.

After about an hour, we were almost finished. That's when I first noticed T. J. Stoner. He was sitting all the way in the back of the room. He was the very last person to tell about himself.

When he got up, he said, "My name is T. J. Stoner. I just moved here from San Diego. I have an older brother who plays baseball for the Chicago Cubs." Then he sat back down and tried to look cool.

Boy, do I hate it when kids try to look cool. I knew right away I wasn't going to like T. J. Stoner.

"That's very interesting, T.J.," said Miss Henderson. You could tell she was really impressed. "Could you tell us a little bit more about yourself?"

"Well, okay." T.J. stood up again. "My brother's name is Matt Stoner, and he plays third base. This is his second year in the majors."

"Do you play baseball, too, T.J.?" asked Miss Henderson.

16

"Yes," said T.J., "I'm a pitcher. Last year my team won the state championship in California. I was voted the Most Valuable Player."

"My goodness!" screeched Miss Henderson. "It really sounds as though you'll be playing for the Cubs someday yourself!"

Yuck! This whole conversation was making me sick! I raised my hand and began waving it all over the place. I could tell that Miss Henderson didn't want to call on me, but I was pretty hard to ignore.

"Yes?" she said, sounding disgusted.

I stood up. "Miss Henderson," I began, "I just thought that the class might like to know that I play baseball, too." She just kept staring at me, with her hands on her hips. I continued. "Last season, I played center field. At the end of the year, I was voted the Player with the Slowest Mother."

The whole class roared. Brenda Ferguson laughed so hard she almost fell off her chair. But two people didn't laugh at all. One was Miss Henderson. The other was T. J. Stoner.

I decided to sit down and keep my mouth shut for a while. The good thing about me is that I usually know when to quit. I may be funny, but I'm not stupid.

chapter three

Sometimes I think it would be fun to be a school principal . . . especially in the summer. A school principal spends his summers making up lists of all the kids in the school who hate each other. Then he makes sure he puts them together in the same class.

He really must have had a good laugh when he put T.J. and me in the same room again this year. Ever since I got sent to the principal for wearing wax lips to music class, he hasn't seemed to like me much.

When I first discovered the bad news about T.J., I hurried to tell my mother. I was hoping that maybe she could call the school and have me switched to a different classroom or something.

But no such luck. All my mother did was tell me that I should try to ignore him. She's always giving me great advice like that. Then she hands me my lunch, shoves me out the door, and her problems are over for the day. Mine are just beginning.

Last year, T. J. Stoner grew to be the biggest kid in the whole fifth grade. When I began to notice how big he was getting, I decided it might not be a bad idea to try to make friends with him. But unfortunately, T.J. didn't seem too interested. If I remember correctly, his exact words were, "Get lost, creep-head."

"Does that mean no?" I asked.

T.J. grabbed me by the shoulders and looked me straight in the eye. Then he said, "It means I hate your guts, Alex!"

"Aw come on, T.J.," I said, smiling. "Can't our guts be friends?"

T.J. didn't think that was quite as funny as I did. I could tell by the way he pushed me down and sat on my head. "Stop being such a jerk, you skinny bag of bones. You're beginning to get on my nerves." He gave me another shove and left. It's too bad my mother wasn't there. Maybe she could have told me how to ignore someone s knee when it's shoved in your mouth.

I think the worst thing about being in the same room with T.J. is having him in my gym class. I hate to admit it, but he's really a great athlete. For a kid, T. J. Stoner is the best baseball player that I've ever seen.

There's only one sport that I'm better at than T.J.—square dancing. I figure I can count square dancing as a sport because we do it in gym. You ought to see me. I can promenade my partner better than any other kid in the whole school.

One time I asked the gym teacher, Mr. Mc-Guinsky, if he ever thought about starting a school square dancing team. I told him that if he did, I would like to volunteer to be the team captain.

He must have thought I was making a joke. He told me to sit my tail down and shut up. Gym teachers like to say "tail" a lot.

I do play other sports besides square dancing. Take Little League for instance. I've been in Little League for six years now. But to tell you the truth, I'm not what you'd call a real good athlete. Actually, I'm not even real fair. I'm more what you'd call real stinky.

I've got proof, too. Every single year that I've

played Little League, I've received the trophy for the Most Improved Player.

You may think that means I'm pretty good. That's what *I* used to think, too. But, over the past six years, I've noticed that none of the really good players ever gets the Most Improved Player award. And I finally figured out why. It's because the good players are already so good that they can't improve much. Let's face it, the only players on a team who can improve are the players who stink to begin with.

Last year, at the end of baseball season, I tried to explain how I felt to my father. We were sitting together at the Little League awards ceremony. The announcer began calling the names of all the players who were going to be receiving trophies.

I started to get very nervous.

"Just relax, Alex," said my father. "It won't be the end of the world if you don't win Most Improved again this year."

He just didn't understand at all.

"That's just it, Dad," I said, trying to explain. "I don't *want* to get Most Improved again. I don't mean to be a poor sport or anything, but if they call my name, why don't we just pretend we're not here. What do you say, Dad?"

I could tell by his face that my father was shocked. "Pretend we're not here!" he said loudly. "What kind of sportsmanship do you call that?"

"Shhh . . . Dad . . . not so loud," I said, trying to quiet him down. "It's just too embarrassing to get *another* Improved award, that's all. I just don't want it."

"I can't believe you!" my father exclaimed. "How ungrateful can you get, Alex? Do you know how many kids here would *love* to get that award tonight?"

"I know, Dad," I answered, "but that's only because most of them haven't figured out what the Most Improved trophy really means. They don't understand that getting that award means that you were *really* a stink-o player at the beginning of the season. Big deal. I'm supposed to be happy because I've gone from being stink-o to just smelly."

About that time, I heard my name being called over the microphone.

"Alex Frankovitch. Most Improved Player award for team number seven, Preston's Pest Control!"

When I heard it, I slid way down in my seat so that no one could see me. I could tell that my

22

father was *very* annoyed with the way I was acting. He kept trying to grab my arm and make me stand up. Instead, I doubled over even further, and put my head between my knees.

The announcer called my name again. "Alex Frankovitch? Is Alex here?' he bellowed.

My father jumped up from his seat and pointed at me. At least that's what I *think* he did. I couldn't be sure. I was too busy trying to wad myself up into a little ball.

"Here he is, right here," screamed my dad. "Alex Frankovitch is right here!"

I guess everyone thought I was just being shy. The next thing I knew, the announcer shouted, "Let's give Alex a little applause to get him down here!"

Everyone started clapping. Then a few of the kids who knew me started shouting, "WE WANT ALEX . . . WE WANT ALEX!"

Finally, I had no choice. I stood up and started making my way down the bleachers. By the time I reached the fifth row, I had decided that I would never speak to my father again.

When I got to the bottom, I spotted T. J. Stoner. He was there getting another Most Valuable Player trophy. He kept pointing at me and laughing . . . pointing and laughing. . . .

I just couldn't let him get away with making fun of me. I decided that the only thing I could do was to pretend that I was really enjoying myself.

I walked to the middle of the gym floor, turned around, and started taking bows and throwing kisses. Then I walked over to the table to pick up my trophy.

The announcer handed me the microphone as I received my award. I was supposed to say thank you. But instead, I took the microphone, held it up to my mouth and burped.

The whole crowd started laughing at once. At least that's the way it sounded. Actually, I think the only people laughing were the kids. Usually, grownups don't think burping is quite as funny as kids do.

After that I decided to walk home. I knew I was in trouble, so I went straight to my room and waited for my father.

While I was waiting, I made a sign and hung it on the outside of my door. The sign said:

THIS ROOM BELONGS TO ALEX FRANKOVITCH,
THE ONLY BOY IN THE WHOLE WORLD
WHO HAS GONE FROM STINK-O TO SMELLY
SIX YEARS IN A ROW.

24

When my father saw the sign, he didn't even bother coming into my room to yell at me. I guess he figured I already felt bad enough.

He was right.

chapter four

For me, the worst part about belonging to Little League is the uniforms. Every year, the same thing happens. This year, at my second practice, it happened again.

The coach makes everyone line up to tell him what size shirt and pants they needed. He calls out a name and we shout out our size. We have three choices: small, medium, or large.

I checked out the other kids on my team. There were twelve of us all together. I figured that out of our whole team there were five larges, six mediums, and one teeny-tiny . . . me.

Every single year I am the smallest kid on the team. For a long time, I actually thought that I was a midget.

I remember when I was in first grade our teacher asked us to cut out magazine pictures of what we thought we would look like when we grew up. Most of the guys in my class brought in pictures of baseball or football players. A couple of others brought in pictures of policemen.

I brought in a picture of a Munchkin.

I got it out of *TV Guide*. Munchkins are the short little guys that keep running all over the place in the movie *The Wizard of Oz*.

I think my teacher was surprised when she saw my picture. She called me up to her desk.

"Alex, what is this a picture of?" she asked.

"It's a Munchkin," I answered.

"That's what I was afraid of," she said.

"Oh, you don't have to be afraid of Munchkins, Mrs. Hurley," I said. "They're too short to hurt anyone."

"I *know* that they're short, Alex," she replied. "What I don't understand is why you want to be one when you grow up."

"I don't," I answered. "I want to be a baseball player."

"Then why did you bring in this picture?" asked Mrs. Hurley.

"Because *that's* what I'm going to look like," I explained. "You said to bring in a picture of what we were going to *look* like, didn't you?"

I guess Mrs. Hurley must have been worried about me. When I got home from school that day, she had already called my mother. As soon as I walked in the door, Mom sat me down and had a nice long talk with me about midgets.

"Alex," said my mother, "I know that you think you're too short. But that's only because you haven't started to grow as much as some of the other kids. Everyone grows at *different* speeds. But, believe me, you are going to grow! You are *not* going to be a Munchkin."

Then she took me by the hand and led me to the kitchen. She stood me up against the wall near the corner and told me not to move.

For a minute I thought she was going to try to shoot an apple off my head or something. Instead, she got a pencil and made a mark on the wall behind me. When I moved away, she wrote the date right next to it.

"Now," she said, "just to prove to you how much you're growing, we will measure you every six months. You won't believe it until you see it."

Well, all I can say is six months is a long time to wait . . . especially when you're waiting to find out whether or not you're a midget.

When the day finally came to measure me again, I was pretty nervous about it.

My mother stood me up against the wall in the same spot where I had been measured before. Then she carefully made another pencil mark. When I turned to look at it, I was *very* relieved. I had grown almost half an inch.

"Now do you believe me?" asked my mother. "Does this prove to you that you're not going to be a Munchkin?"

"Yeah, I guess so," I answered. "Now, if I could only figure out a way to put on some weight."

My mother threw her hands in the air. "I give up!" she shouted. "Honestly, Alex, if it's not one problem, it's another!" Then she just shook her head and left the room.

Sometimes my mother doesn't understand me at all. Being small is not an easy thing to be. Especially when you have to shout it out in front of your whole entire baseball team.

"Alex Frankovitch?" yelled my coach. "Small, medium, or large?"

I just couldn't bring myself to say "small." In fact, I guess you could say I panicked.

"Large!" I shouted.

Everyone on the team turned around to look at me. A couple of them laughed.

The coach walked over to me.

"Did you say 'large,' Alex?" he asked.

"Yes sir," I answered. "Large."

"Are you *sure* that large is the size you take, Alex?" he asked.

"Oh, no sir," I answered. "I usually don't take a large."

The coach looked relieved. "Well, what size do you usually take?"

"Extra large," I answered.

He just looked at me for a minute and then scribbled something down on his paper. As he walked away he mumbled something to himself that sounded a lot like "bubble-head." But I really didn't care what he thought. At least I didn't have to shout out "small" in front of the whole team.

I figured that the day the uniforms came would be the best day of my entire life. I even had a dream about it.

In my dream, the coach had all the uniforms arranged in two piles . . . small and large.

Then he stood up and began calling out our names and sizes. When your name and size were called, you were supposed to go to the correct pile and select your uniform.

"Alex Frankovitch . . . large!" he shouted, loud enough for everyone to hear.

Slowly, I stood up and walked over to the large pile to choose my pants and shirt. When I got there, I realized that my uniform was the only one in the large pile. Everyone else on my team was a small. As I reached down to pick up my large shirt, everyone started to clap.

It was the best dream I ever had.

Finally, after waiting for three whole weeks for my dream to come true, the team uniforms came in. I was so excited I could hardly stand it.

When I got to practice that day, I noticed that the coach had arranged the uniforms in three piles. My heart started pounding wildly. It was almost like my dream. I felt like I had seen into the future or something.

Everyone lined up and the coach told us to go to the correct pile and pick out a uniform. This wasn't quite as good as if he had called out my name and size, but I really didn't mind. All I really cared about was having everyone see me at the large pile.

As soon as it was my turn, I rushed over and grabbed a large shirt and a pair of pants. I hung around the pile for a few seconds so everyone could see me, and then I took my uniform and stood back so the other kids could get theirs. When all the piles were gone, the coach told us to

31

check our uniforms to make sure we had chosen the right size.

All of a sudden, I heard a few of the guys start to laugh. I turned around and saw Randy Tubbs trying to pull his new shirt over his head. It was stuck on his ears. Randy Tubbs is the biggest kid on our team. His head probably weighs as much as my entire body.

"Hey, Coach," he shouted, "I think I've got a little problem here!"

The coach walked over and helped Randy get the shirt off his head. Then he looked inside to see what size it was.

"This is a small, Randy," he said. "You ordered a large."

"Yeah," said Randy, "but this was the only uniform left when I got there."

The coach started looking all around. All of a sudden, I got this real sick feeling in my stomach. I tried to sneak off the practice field, but as I was walking away, he spotted me.

"Hold it, Alex," said the coach. "Bring your uniform over here for a minute, would you?"

As I handed the coach my shirt and pants, I checked the tag. "See, Coach? It's a large, just like you ordered for me," I said.

"Alex, I ordered you a small," he said. Then

he gave my uniform to Randy and handed me the small.

Boy, did that ever make me mad. What gave him the right to steal my uniform like that?

Randy held up his new shirt. "Now *that's* better!" he said, smiling.

When I got home I tried on my uniform. I sure didn't have any trouble getting it over my head. Good old Randy had really stretched the neck out of shape. It hung down to my stomach!

My mother told me not to worry about it. She said the shirt would probably shrink a little when it was washed. I didn't tell her, but I wished the pants would shrink too. They were way too big.

chapter five

T. J. Stoner brags about his baseball team more than any kid I've ever known in my whole life. So what if his team hasn't lost a game all year? It doesn't mean they won just because of T.J. Everyone knows that one kid can't make the difference between a winning team and a losing team. After all, every team *I've* ever been on has come in last place. And I don't care what anyone says, all those teams didn't lose just because of me.

This year I happen to know that I am not the worst player on my team. The worst player on my team is Ryan Brady. Ryan doesn't help us out at all. The very first game of the season, Ryan broke his arm. Now all he does is sit on the bench. I'm sure I help the team out a lot more than Ryan.

I play center field. A lot of kids think that if you play in the outfield, it means you stink. My father says that's ridiculous. He says that outfielders are just as important as infielders. He told me that when he was a boy, he played in the outfield just like me. But that doesn't really make me feel much better. I've seen my father play baseball. He stinks.

My mother says that when people like T. J. Stoner brag, it's just because they're trying to get attention. And, as usual, she says to ignore them. But, for some reason, whenever I hear T.J. start to brag about his baseball team, I just can't seem to keep my mouth shut.

One day, a couple of weeks ago, I heard him talking to a bunch of kids out on the playground.

"My coach told me that for a kid, I was the best pitcher he had ever seen in his life," he said.

When I heard *that*, I did a very dumb thing. I called over to my friend Brian Dunlop. "Hey, Brian," I shouted, "I forgot to tell you. Last night, at baseball practice, my coach let me pitch. And boy, was he impressed! He said that I threw the fastest ball he had ever seen!"

I *know* it was a ridiculous thing to say, but

Brian sure wasn't much help. When he heard what I was saying, he fell on the ground and started laughing. I guess I really couldn't blame him, though. Brian has seen me throw.

Pretty soon, T.J. came strolling over. He bent over to talk to Brian. "Did I hear Skinnybones say that he can throw a fast ball?"

Brian couldn't stop laughing long enough to answer, so he just nodded his head.

T.J. stood up and walked over to where I was standing. "Hey, Frankovitch," he said, "I'll make you a little deal."

"Gee, I'm sorry, T.J.," I answered, shaking my head. "If you're going to try and get me to come pitch for your team, you're too late. The Yankees already called me this morning."

Brian let out another wild scream of laughter. T.J. joined him. I guess the idea of me pitching was even funnier than I thought.

One time I tried pitching with my dad. But it really didn't work out very well. Most of the balls I threw didn't even make it to the plate. Eight of them bounced in the dirt. The only ball that made it over the plate beaned him on the head.

"What kind of a stupid pitch was that?" shouted my father as he rubbed his head.

"I call it my old bean ball!" I shouted back.

I guess he wasn't in the mood for jokes that day. We packed up our stuff and went home.

Anyway, after T.J. finally stopped laughing about my big offer from the Yankees, he started bugging me again.

"Come on, Alex," he begged, "just listen to my deal. What have you got to lose?"

By this time a bunch of kids had started to gather around us. I think most of them had come over to see what was wrong with Brian.

"Okay, T.J.," I said, "tell me your deal. But make it snappy. It's almost time for Brian to massage my pitching arm."

"Okay," said T.J. "This is it. Since we're both such good pitchers, let's hold a contest after school to see who's the best. We'll even get a couple of kids to be the official umpires. What do you say, Frankovitch, is it a deal or not?"

Geez, what a mess I was in! If I said no, everyone would think I was chicken. But, if I said yes, everyone would be able to see how badly I pitched. I just had to get out of it!

I thought about it for a couple of minutes before I answered. "Gee, I'd really *love* to, T.J.," I answered finally. "But my coach told me not to tire my arm out by being in any stupid pitching contests. Thanks anyway."

I started to walk away but T.J. grabbed me by the shoulders. "You get one of your friends, Frankovitch, and I'll get one of mine. They'll be the umps. I'll meet you at the Little League field after school. If you're not there, we'll all know it's just because you're chicken."

As he turned to walk away, he stopped and looked back at me. "Be there, creep-head!" he shouted.

After he was gone, I looked down at Brian. He was still on the ground.

"Hey, Brian," I said, "how would you like to be an umpire this afternoon?"

Brian nodded his head. I think his sides were still hurting from all that laughing.

I reached my hand out to help him up. Together, we started back to class.

"Geez, Brian," I said, "if you think this is funny, wait until you see me pitch."

Then both of us started laughing. I figured I'd better laugh now while I had the chance.

chapter six

I was hoping the afternoon would drag on and on, but before I knew it the three o'clock bell rang. My teacher, Mrs. Grayson, dismissed the class.

I didn't want to go.

"Listen, Mrs. Grayson," I said, as she was getting ready to leave. "How would you like some help cleaning the boards and erasers this afternoon?"

"No thanks, Alex," she replied, "I've got a meeting to go to."

"Mrs. Grayson!" I said, trying to sound shocked, "I'm surprised at you! Do you mean to tell me that you are actually going to leave the room looking like a pig pen?"

"Please, Alex," she replied, "no jokes, okay? I'm really in a hurry." She held the door open for me to leave.

"Exactly what kind of meeting are you going to, Mrs. Grayson?" I asked.

"It's just a teachers' meeting, Alex, that's all. But I don't want to be late, so let's go, huh?"

"Listen, Mrs. Grayson," I continued. "How would you like it if I came along with you? That way, if the meeting got real boring, we could play tic-tac-toe, or something."

Mrs. Grayson stopped rushing me out the door. "Alex, is there some *reason* that you don't want to leave school today?" she asked. "Are you in some sort of trouble?"

"Trouble? Me?" I answered. "Oh no, Mrs. Grayson. Not me! I was just trying to make your meeting a little more fun, that's all."

"Well, thanks anyway, Alex," she said, "but I think I'll be able to stay awake today."

"Okay, have it your own way," I said, "but don't say I didn't try to help. I guess I'll just be heading on home now, Mrs. Grayson. That is, unless you'd like me to stick around until after your meeting's over to help you erase the boards. . . ."

I think Mrs. Grayson was getting a little

annoyed with me. "Go home, Alex!" she shouted.

So I did. I went home and got my ball and glove. Then I called Brian and told him to meet me at the Little League field.

By the time I got there, everyone else was already waiting for the contest to begin. And, when I say everyone, I mean *everyone*. There must have been about a million kids standing around waiting for me to make a big fool out of myself.

"Hey, Frankovitch!" shouted T.J., when he saw me coming. "For a minute there, I didn't think you were going to show up. What took you so long? Were you home plucking your feathers?"

I think this was his way of calling me a chicken again.

"A turkey like you probably knows a lot about feathers, T.J.!" I shouted back.

A few of the kids standing around started to laugh. T.J. wasn't one of them. He walked over to me.

"This is what we're going to do, Frankovitch," he began, seriously. "I brought along a catcher. He'll be catching for both of us."

I looked over at the kid in the catcher's mask. It was Hank Grover, one of T.J.'s best friends.

"Not fair! Not fair!" I protested. "I should have gotten to bring my own catcher, too!"

"What difference does it make who catches?" he asked. "The catcher isn't going to call balls or strikes. The umpires are going to do that. And besides, Alex," he added, "none of your jerky little friends knows how to catch."

Boy, did that ever make me mad! Insulting my friends like that! I probably should have punched him right in the mouth. Except for one tiny little problem. He was right. None of my jerky little friends *can* catch.

"Okay," T.J. continued, "we're each going to pitch ten balls. Your umpire and my umpire will stand together behind home plate. Then, as each ball is thrown, they will decide whether it's a strike or a ball. And to make it fair, the umpires *have* to agree on every call. If they can't agree, the pitcher takes the whole thing over again. Does that seem fair to you, Frankovitch?"

"Yeah, I guess so," I said. By this time I was getting nervous. All I *really* wanted to do was go home.

T.J. took a dime out of his pocket. "We'll flip to see who gets to pitch first," he said.

"Gee, I'm really sorry, T.J.," I said. "But I guess we won't be able to have this contest after all. I never learned how to flip. Maybe we could just somersault to see who goes first."

"Very funny. Now, heads or tails?" he yelled as he threw the coin in the air.

"Tummies," I hollered, trying to look very serious.

"Listen, Alex!" he yelled. "Knock off the funny stuff. Now . . . I'm going to toss this up one more time—heads or tails?" he shouted again.

I called tails.

It was heads. A bad sign.

"Okay," said T.J., "I won the toss, so I'll go first."

He took his ball and glove to the pitcher's mound. T.J.'s umpire, Eddie Fowler, and my umpire, Brian, took their places behind home plate. I hated to admit it, but having two umpires really did seem very fair. The trouble was, it seemed a little too fair. Before T.J. started pitching, I decided to have a little talk with Brian. I called him over.

"Listen, Brian," I said, "just because T. J. Stoner happens to be the very best pitcher that we've ever seen, doesn't mean that he's *perfect*. So, whatever you do, don't be afraid to call one of his pitches a ball if you really think it's a ball. And I

43

don't want you to think that I would ever try to get you to cheat or anything, but keep in mind that I will be glad to pay you a dime for every ball you call—"

T.J. saw me talking to Brian and shouted, "Hey, Alex, don't bother trying to get Brian to cheat for you. I told him before you got here that if I caught him cheating, I'd break his face."

Brian looked at me and smiled. "Sorry, Alex," he said, "but I think I'd rather keep my face than make a couple of lousy dimes."

I was doomed.

T.J. was all set. "I'm ready!" he shouted.

"Ready?" I yelled back. "Aren't we even going to get a couple of practice pitches or anything?"

"You can practice if you *need* to, Frankovitch," he hollered, "but I don't really want any."

T.J. went into his windup. Some kids look dumb when they're winding up. But T.J. looked just like Steve Carlton.

Then he threw. The ball hit the catcher's mitt at about sixty miles an hour. But even worse, it hit his glove *exactly* in the center.

"Strike one!" shouted both umpires together.

T.J. didn't even blink an eye. He just got ready to throw the next pitch.

"Strike two!" shouted the umpires as the

second pitch crossed the middle of the plate.

This time, T.J. looked over in my direction and smiled. I leaned down and pretended I was tying my shoe so I wouldn't have to look at him.

"What's the matter, Alex?" he shouted. "Is the ball flying by so fast that it's untying your shoes?"

Then he laughed and got ready for his third pitch. As usual, it was perfect. The guy was really beginning to make me sick.

Every single pitch he threw came whizzing over the plate so fast you could hardly even see it. The catcher never even had to move a muscle. The ball hit the center of his mitt ten times straight! It was really disgusting.

"Okay, Skinnybones," he yelled after he'd thrown his last pitch, "it's your turn."

As T.J. sat down on the sidelines, Brian walked over and patted me on the back.

"Some friend you turned out to be, Brian," I said angrily. "What's the matter, did you forget how to say the word 'ball'?"

"Oh, get off it, Alex," he answered. "All his pitches were perfect. You really didn't expect me to cheat, did you?"

"Great, Brian," I said. "I'll remember how you feel about cheating the next time you need help on a math test."

Then I grabbed my glove and slowly walked out to the pitcher's mound. I was hoping that maybe, if I walked slowly enough, it would be dark by the time I got there and everyone would have to go home to dinner. But unfortunately, when I got to the mound the sun was still shining. There was no getting out of it now. I took a deep breath and turned around.

Oh no! It was a lot farther to home plate than I remembered. I began to panic. I can't throw all the way from here! I thought to myself. I'm so far away, the two umpires look like midgets!

Just then the two umpires stood up. Whew! That was a close one. They must have sat down when they saw how long it was taking me to get out to the mound.

The umpires lined up behind home plate and the catcher got set.

"Are you ready yet, Skinnybones?" yelled T.J. "Or do you want to practice first?"

Aha! A perfect opportunity to stall for time! Slowly, I walked off the mound and headed for T.J. on the sidelines. As soon as I got there he stood up. I stood on tiptoe and tried to look him in the eye.

"For your information, T.J.," I said, trying to act tough, "there is nothing skinny about my bones. So I would appreciate it if you would stop calling me that stupid name."

T.J. grabbed hold of my arm and held it up next to his.

"If your bones aren't skinny," he said, "then why is my arm so much bigger than yours?"

"You've got fat skin," I said simply.

T.J.'s eyes started getting real squinty. That meant he was about to hit me, so I hurried back out to the mound before he had a chance.

I stood there for a few minutes trying to figure out how to begin my windup. But pretty soon some of the kids started shouting at me to hurry up. So finally I was forced to begin.

I pulled my glove back toward my chest and stared at the catcher's mitt. Then I raised my left leg high in the air and hopped on my right foot.

Both of the umpires started to giggle. The catcher fell right over in the dirt laughing. They didn't even give me a chance to throw.

"Time out!" I yelled. "No fair! Interference on the umpires and the catcher!"

For once in his life, T.J. seemed to agree with me. He went over and tried to get the three of them to calm down. It took a few minutes, but finally they got themselves under control.

Once again, I went into my windup. I pulled

my glove back to my chest, raised my left leg high into the air, hopped on my right foot, and let the ball go.

I watched carefully as it rolled all the way to the plate. Wow! I thought to myself. What a pitch! It was a little low, of course, but at least I had it going in the right direction.

"Ball one!" shouted both umpires together.

"Well, I guess that's it, T.J.," I called as I walked off the mound. "I lost. One little mistake on my first pitch and it's all over. There's no way I can win, or even tie your pitching record when I've already got a ball. It's really a shame, too. That's probably the only bad pitch I'd have thrown all day."

"Not so fast, Frankovitch!" screamed T.J., running after me. He caught up to me and grabbed me by the collar. "You have nine more balls to throw, hot shot. We had a deal. So get back to that mound and we'll just see how good you are."

I knew there was no sense trying to argue with him. So slowly I turned around and headed back. Maybe there's still hope, I thought. If only I could throw a couple of good solid strikes, just one or two, at least I wouldn't end up looking like such an idiot.

I took a deep breath and got ready to throw my second pitch. My windup was the same, but something terrible happened when I started to throw. As I took the ball behind my head, it slipped out of my hand and landed in the dirt three feet behind me.

By this time I had really had it. All I wanted to do was get the whole thing over with quickly so I could go home and die. Brian had fallen in the dirt laughing. His mouth formed the words "Ball two," but nothing came out. I wound up and threw my third pitch as hard as I could.

T.J. was still watching from the sidelines. Unfortunately, my aim was a little bit off and the ball hit him in the arm.

"Strike one!" I shouted myself.

T.J. came running over holding his arm. "What do you mean, strike one?" he demanded, grabbing my shirt.

"Well, it struck you, didn't it?" I said, giggling.

"Let's see how you like being struck, Skinny-bones," he yelled, punching my arm as hard as he could.

Then he punched me again.

"Just remember what this feels like the next time you want to hit me with a ball," he growled. Somehow I got the feeling the contest was over.

My arm was a goner. It just hung limp at my side like it had croaked or something. I checked it out to see if it was bleeding, but no such luck. I hate that. When something hurts as bad as my arm did, the least it could do is bleed a little.

As T.J. walked away a lot of kids started running after him. Most of them were patting him on the arm and telling him what a great pitcher he was.

It's a good thing I didn't win. If anyone had patted me on my arm, I'm sure it would have fallen right off into the dirt.

I waited around a few minutes to walk home with Brian, but he must have left without me. At first I was mad about it, but in a way I understood. I guess he was just too embarrassed to walk home with a loser. I knew exactly how he felt. I didn't want to walk home with me, either.

chapter seven

Sometimes I wonder why I even bother to play baseball at all. I hate the uniforms, I can't throw, and I don't like playing center field. Lately I've been giving this a lot of thought, and there's only one thing I can come up with. . . .

I play for the caps.

Baseball caps are probably the greatest invention of all time. No matter what you look like, as soon as you put on a baseball cap you look just like Steve Garvey. Even my cat looks like Steve Garvey with my cap on.

Once I did an experiment with my grandmother just to prove it. My grandmother's about eighty years old, but she doesn't look it. She doesn't need a cane and she only wears glasses when she reads.

One of the things I like best about my grandmother is her blue hair. It's just about the coolest hair I've ever seen. I'm not sure that she really knows it's blue. I think she might be a little bit color-blind. One time at dinner she told my mother that she puts a "steel gray" rinse on it. I started to tell her that it looked more like "steel blue," but my mother stuck a roll in my mouth.

Anyway, after we finished eating that night, I ran up to my room and grabbed my baseball cap. Then I snuck up behind my grandmother and put it on her head. Just as I thought! Another Steve Garvey!

My grandmother wasn't a very good sport about it. She pulled my cap off her head and dropped it on the floor. Boy, I had really messed up her blue hair! In fact it was so messy that, right at the top of her head, I noticed a little bald spot. I offered to let her put my cap back on but she ignored me. I really felt sorry for her. She must have gone to the same barber I go to. My barber, Mr. Peoples, has given me more bald spots than I can even count.

I'll never forget the time he made my head look like a grapefruit. As soon as I walked in his shop that day, I knew I was in trouble. I always think it's a good idea to find out what kind of mood Mr. Peoples is in before I sit down in his chair. Sometimes when barbers aren't feeling very happy, they like to give kids funny haircuts to cheer themselves up.

"Hi, Mr. Peoples," I said with a smile. "How are you feeling today?"

Mr. Peoples looked at me and frowned. "I'll tell you how I'm feeling," he growled. "I'm hot, tired, and hungry. Any more questions?"

"Ah . . . no, Mr. Peoples, no more questions," I said as I began backing out of his shop. "Gee, I think I hear my mother calling. Maybe I'd better come back tomorrow."

"Knock it off, Alex, and sit down," he ordered, giving me a real disgusted look. Mr. Peoples has known me since I was two, so he thinks he can talk to me like that.

"Are you positive you want me to sit down?" I asked. "I mean, if you're not in a good mood I'd be happy to leave you alone for a little while."

"Sit!" he said gruffly, pointing to the chair.

Slowly I climbed into the big red seat. "Well, okay," I agreed. "But I really don't need a big haircut. I'd just like you to take a little bit off the sides. Okay?"

Mr. Peoples didn't hear a word I said. He was too busy plugging in his electric clippers.

"Wait a minute, Mr. Peoples!" I said quickly. "Do you really think you need the clippers today? I just want a little trim, remember?"

"Who's the barber here, Alex, you or me?" he asked sharply.

That's when I decided to be quiet. If there was one thing I didn't want to do, it was make the guy any madder than he already was.

Mr. Peoples started clipping. No wait . . . clipping is the wrong word. Mr. Peoples started scalping.

"You would have made a great Indian, Mr. Peoples," I said. But the clippers were so loud, he didn't hear me.

He whizzed those loud buzzing clippers all around the back of my head and headed up toward my ears.

All of a sudden, I heard him say, "Whoopsie!"

"Whoopsie?" I asked, nervously. "Did you just say 'whoopsie,' Mr. Peoples?"

I looked in the mirror. Right over my left ear, I saw the 'whoopsie.' It was a big round bald spot.

"This may be just a little bit shorter than you wanted it, Alex," said Mr. Peoples. "But at least it will be nice and cool for the summer."

"Nice and cool?" I asked angrily. "How do you figure that? If there are any more 'whoopsies' I'll have to spend the whole summer wearing a big brown bag over my head. Have you ever spent the summer in a paper bag, Mr. Peoples?"

"Look on the bright side, Alex," he replied. "Think how easy it will be to take care of. Instead of combing through a lot of hair, all you'll have to do is polish your head a little." Then he laughed.

I couldn't stand to look in the mirror anymore so I closed my eyes and waited until he was finished. After circling my head with the clippers about twenty more times, he finally shut them off.

Slowly I opened my eyes and looked into the mirror. I couldn't believe it! I've seen more hair on an egg! I turned my head and looked at it from every angle hoping to find hair. But it was all gone.

"How do you like it?" asked Mr. Peoples, handing me a mirror.

"How do I like what?" I growled.

"Your hair, of course," he answered.

I gazed down at the floor. "I liked it a lot better when it was on my head," I replied as Mr. Peoples got the broom and started to sweep my hair into the dustpan.

He laughed. "I guess that means you think it's a little too short, huh?"

"No, Mr. Peoples," I answered. "If it was too short, at least some of it would still be growing out of my head. I'd say it's too gone."

He laughed again. "That will be five dollars," he said, holding out his hand.

I slapped the money down and ran home as fast as I could. My mother met me at the door.

"Look what that butcher did to me!" I yelled, pointing to my head.

My mother stared at me for a minute. I could tell she was having a hard time trying not to laugh. "Don't worry," she said, finally getting control of herself. "The good thing about hair is that it always grows back."

"Yeah well, that might be the good thing about hair," I snapped, "but what's the good thing about no hair?"

My mother started to giggle. Then she turned and left the room.

"Where are you going?" I yelled. "You've got to help me figure out what to do with all this scalp!"

"I'll be right back," she answered, still snickering. "I'm just going to the kitchen for a minute.

All of a sudden I have this tremendous craving for grapefruit."

"Very funny!" I screamed at her. "Very, very funny!"

Anyway, right after that I remembered about my baseball cap. I hurried up to my room to find it. I opened up my closet and breathed a sigh of relief. For once I had remembered to put it back on the hook where it belonged. I put it on my head and it slipped down a little bit. Being bald makes your head a lot thinner. I looked in the mirror. Yup. Just like old Steve Garvey! It works every time.

I just wish that putting on a baseball cap could make me hit home runs like Steve Garvey. I guess you could say that hitting a home run is sort of a dream of mine. I don't think it will ever come true, though. My father says that it's pretty hard to hit a home run when all you can do is bunt.

I've always thought "bunt" was a stupid word. The first time I heard it I was only about seven. This kid on my baseball team was on his way up to bat. Before he left the bench, he turned around and said to me, "I think I'm going to bunt."

At first I didn't really know what he was

talking about, but whatever it was, it didn't sound too good. I tried to figure out what he meant, and finally decided that "bunt" was probably another word for "puke."

Oh no, I thought to myself, that kid's sick and no one even knows it! I got off the bench and went running over to the coach and told him that I thought the kid was going to start bunting any minute.

"That's okay, Alex," said the coach, "don't worry about it. I *told* him to bunt."

Now, I was really confused. Why in the world would a coach tell one of his players to throw up? What kind of a trick was this? I hoped he wouldn't tell me to bunt, too.

"Listen, Coach," I said, "I don't think I could bunt even if I wanted to. I feel pretty good and I haven't even eaten dinner yet."

The coach looked at me kind of funny and told me to sit down. I went back to the bench and watched the kid at bat. I wondered when he was going to do it. When the ball came, he took his bat and held it out to the side. I figured he was just trying to get it out of the way so he didn't bunt on it. Since I was next at bat, I thought this was a pretty nice thing to do.

But, instead of getting sick, the kid took the

bat and lightly knocked the ball down the third baseline. He ran as fast as he could and made it to first base in plenty of time.

"Great bunt!" shouted the coach.

I turned to the boy sitting next to me. "I didn't see him bunt. Where is it?"

"Where is what?" he asked.

"You know," I said. "Where is the bunt?"

"Weren't you watching?" he asked. "He just bunted the ball down the third baseline and then ran to first."

Suddenly, I knew what a bunt really was. Brother, did I ever feel like an idiot! Thank goodness no one ever knew what I had been talking about.

Anyway, from that day on, I started working on my bunting. And after four years of practice, I'm probably the best bunter in the entire Little League. I guess that's because no one else bothers working on it very much.

Sometimes Brian helps me practice my bunting at recess. Last week, T.J. saw me and walked over.

"Bunting's for sissies," he said, grinning.

I ignored him.

"Anybody with half a muscle can hit the ball hard," he said.

I still ignored him.

"Hey, Skinnybones, I just thought of something," he said with a smile. "Only runts bunt! Get it? It rhymes!"

That's when I decided to stop ignoring him. Brian pitched me another ball. I held the bat out until the very last minute. Then I turned it sharply so that the ball hit T.J. right on the head.

"Whoops! Sorry there, T.J.," I said. "It seems that all I've been doing lately is accidentally hitting you with baseballs. It's a good thing *that* one hit you on the head. Otherwise, you might have gotten hurt."

T.J. walked over, shoved me to the ground, and pounced on top of me. "Well, Mr. Skinnybones, we'll just see how good you bunt on Saturday," he said.

"What happens on Saturday?" I asked. But T.J. didn't understand me. It's hard to speak clearly when your mouth is full of someone's leg.

Then I remembered. Saturday was the day when our Little League teams were scheduled to play each other.

chapter eight

Usually, when I go to the Little League field for a game, I don't know who we're going to play until I get there. I just go to the game, lose, and go home. The way I look at it, losing is losing. Who cares who you lose *to*?

A lot of kids don't feel that way. T.J. is one of them. He's one of those kids who *always* knows exactly which team he's playing, and what their record is. Then, a couple of days before they play, he goes around telling the whole world how the other team is going to get creamed. And the trouble is . . . they know it's true.

The day before we played his team, T.J. went all over the playground shouting out that Franklin's Sporting Goods was going to "mop up the floor" with Fran and Ethel's Cleaning Service.

Fran and Ethel's Cleaning Service—that's the name of my team this year. Neat, huh? When I first found out about it, I thought about quitting. But my father explained to me that Fran and Ethel had paid a lot of money to sponsor our team and that it wouldn't be fair if everyone quit just because it was a stupid name.

So far, I've never had a team name that sounded as neat as Franklin's Sporting Goods. Last year my team was called Preston's Pest Control. Our shirts had pictures of little dead bugs all over them. It was really embarrassing.

Anyway, about five minutes after we got to school on Friday, T.J. raised his hand. When the teacher called on him, he stood up.

"I have an important announcement to make," he said. He looked over at me and smiled. "Tomorrow, at 10:30 A.M., my Little League team is going to be playing Fran and Ethel's Cleaning Service. And, since there are two players in this room that will be playing in that game, I just thought that everyone might enjoy seeing it."

Quickly I raised my hand. I just couldn't let T.J. get away with this. My team hadn't won a game all season, and T.J.'s was in first place. It was going to be humiliating.

The teacher called on me.

"*I* wouldn't," I said.

"You wouldn't what?" asked the teacher with a puzzled look on her face.

"I wouldn't enjoy seeing it," I answered.

"Then don't come," she said simply.

"Thank you, Mrs. Grayson," I said. Then, I sat down with a big fat smile on my face.

T.J. jumped out of his seat. "He *has* to come, Mrs. Grayson! He's playing in the game! If he doesn't show I'll be the only one from our class playing!"

"Okay, then," I said, after the teacher called on me again, "I guess it's all settled. Since there's only *one* kid from our class playing, all the rest of us will stay home and watch cartoons. Tomorrow, *Wolfman Meets the Super Heroes* is on."

By this time, Mrs. Grayson was pretty confused so she dropped the whole thing. But T.J. didn't. As a matter of fact, he talked about it all day long. After school he even stood at the door as the kids were leaving the classroom. As they passed him, he said, "See you at the big game, tomorrow. Don't forget . . . it starts at 10:30!

"See you tomorrow, chicken," he laughed as I tried to sneak past him.

"Who are you calling chicken?" I demanded.

T.J. grabbed me by the shirt and pulled me

right up to his face. "You. That's who," he said, holding tight.

"I don't mean to be rude, T.J.," I said, "but would you mind putting me down? I don't think two people are supposed to be this close unless they're dancing."

T.J. loosened his grip. "Okay, Frankovitch. We'll just see how funny you are tomorrow at the game." Then he smiled and walked away.

Brother, was I ever in for it now! I didn't know what I was going to do. If there's one thing worse than losing, it's losing in front of your whole class.

I've never even played a Little League game in front of a crowd. With a team like mine, you're lucky if even a couple of parents show up. In fact, I hate to admit this, but there are only two people that have shown up at every single game we've played this year . . . Fran and Ethel. They always come to watch us play right after they get off from work. You can tell who they are because they usually stand around wringing out their mops while we warm up.

Anyway, Friday night before the big game, I couldn't sleep at all. I just lay in bed trying to think of a way to get out of playing. I guess I must have thought about it most of the night. But finally, about three o'clock in the morning, I came up with a wonderful idea. I only hoped it would work.

When I went down to breakfast the next morning, I dragged myself into the kitchen on my stomach.

"Good morning, Mom and Dad," I said as I pulled myself over to the breakfast table.

My parents looked down at me on the floor and smiled. "Good morning, Alex," they said together.

"What will you have for breakfast?" asked my mother.

"Cornflakes," I answered, looking up at her.

My mother got up from the table and poured me a bowl of cereal. She stepped over me to get to the refrigerator.

"Juice?" she asked.

I nodded. What was wrong with these people? Didn't they notice that something was wrong with me?

My mother put my breakfast on the floor in front of me. "Better hurry and eat, honey," she said. "You'll have to be dressing for your game soon."

I pushed the cereal and juice out of my way. Then, slowly, I pulled myself over to the table.

When I got there, I pulled my body up into my seat. This whole thing took about ten minutes.

"I think I'd rather eat up here," I said. "Could someone please get me my cornflakes and juice?"

"We're eating right now, Alex," said my dad. "You should have brought your food with you."

Slowly (even slower than before), I leaned down until my hands were on the floor again. The chair flipped over as my body dropped back down. My parents didn't even bother to look up. They were actually ignoring the fact that I couldn't walk!

Finally, I decided to do something really big to get their attention. I pulled myself over to my bowl and started eating my cereal without a spoon. I just put my head in my bowl and started chewing!

After a few minutes of this, my mother walked over to me and dropped a napkin on my head. "You'll probably need this to clean up."

"What kind of parents are you, anyway?" I shouted. "Your poor little son can't walk, and you stand around dropping napkins on his head! Don't you even want to know what happened to me?"

"We already know what happened to you," said my mother calmly

"You mean that you know about how Ronnie Williams ran over my poor legs with his motorbike last night? And you know about how they stiffened up while I was sleeping? And about how they won't work anymore?"

"No, Alex," my mom said. "We know that your whole class is going to be at your baseball game today. Dad and I will be there, too. Brian's parents called this morning, and we're going over to the game with them."

"Oh," I said quietly.

I finished my cereal on the floor. Then I silently pulled myself back out of the kitchen and down the hallway to my room. Sometimes, when you're caught doing something dumb, you feel too embarrassed to stop doing it right away.

When I got back to my room, I stood up and took my uniform out of the drawer. I put on the shirt. The neck still hung down to my stomach. This was going to be the worst day of my life.

chapter nine

Finally, I decided to head over to the Little League field. As I got close enough to see the baseball diamond, I noticed something very unusual. All around the field, the bleachers were packed with people. And when I say packed, I mean *packed*!

"Whew!" I said feeling a million times better. "Thank goodness! It looks like the high school must be having their graduation here this morning. It must be some sort of mix-up. Now, I won't have to play after all!"

I jumped high into the air. "Yeehaa!" I screeched. As I turned around to head for home, I noticed that the Channel Six News truck was parked alongside the curb.

Wow! I thought to myself. This must really be something *big*. It's even going to be on TV. Then I saw a cameraman get out of the truck.

"Hi," I called to him. "Are you going to put that graduation over there on the news tonight?"

"What graduation?" asked the man. "That's no graduation . . . that's a baseball game."

"A baseball game?" I squeaked.

"Yeah," he continued, "there are two Little League teams playing over there this morning We're going to film a few minutes of the game to put on the sports news tonight."

"Gee, mister," I said, taking a deep breath. "This must really be an important game to make the weekend sports. What is it . . . the championship or something?"

"Nope," said the cameraman. "It's nothing like that. As a matter of fact, I think that one of these teams I'm going to be filming hasn't won a game all season."

"I'm doomed!" I hollered. Then I flopped down on the curb and put my head in my hands.

"Are you all right?" he asked.

"All right?" I shouted back. "All right? Of course I'm not all right! What kind of man are you anyway, mister? What kind of a person would want to embarrass a poor rotten Little League team by showing it on the six o'clock news? What's wrong with you? Do you get your kicks making fun of little kids, or what?"

"Wait a minute there, son," he said. "Calm down. I didn't come to make fun of anyone. It's the other team we're interested in. The one with T J. Stoner on it. He's the kid we're doing the story on."

"T.J.?" I asked.

"Yep," he explained. "Yesterday we learned that T. J. Stoner has won every single Little League game he's ever played in. That's a record! In fact, if his team wins today, it will be his 125th straight winning game." I just turned and headed toward the field. As I walked away, the cameraman called after me, "Hey, kid, are you going to be playing in that game?"

"Yeah," I yelled. "I'll be the kid fainting in center field."

What else could go wrong? I looked up into the sky. Maybe now was the time to have a little chat with God. After all, that's what he's there for, isn't it?

"Listen, God," I shouted, "if I did something to make you mad, I'm really sorry. And I'll try never to do it again, whatever it is. But right now, I need your help. I'm a good kid, God. Well . . . pretty good. And I really don't think I deserve this. So I'd like to talk to you about making a little deal.

"If you get all those people sitting in the bleachers to go home right now, I'll become a preacher when I grow up. Would you like that, God?"

I looked around to see if anyone was getting up to leave. No luck. In fact, even more people were coming.

"Okay, God," I said, "if you didn't like that deal, how about this one. All you have to do is get rid of the cameraman. If he goes home, I promise to go to church every single Sunday for the rest of my life."

I looked behind me. The cameraman was carrying all his equipment down to the field. He didn't turn around.

"All right, God," I said one last time. "This is my final offer, and it's a good one. All you have to do is whip up one tiny little thunderstorm to get the game canceled and, in return, I will go home this very minute and read the Bible from cover to cover. How's that?"

I looked into the sky. It was the sunniest, clearest day I had seen in months.

"Thanks, God," I said. "Thanks a whole lot. I know I'm not important like Moses or anything, but I really didn't think it would hurt you to do one tiny little miracle."

When I finally got to the field, my team was already there warming up. Every time I looked into the bleachers my knees turned to jelly. I wasn't sure how long they were going to be able to hold me up.

My coach spotted me.

"Frankovitch," my coach shouted when he spotted me, "where in the heck have you been? Get out there in the field and warm up!"

I trotted out to center field.

"Okay, Alex," he hollered, "I'm going to hit you a couple out there. Get ready."

The first ball he hit me was a high pop fly. I was *very* nervous. It seemed like all the people in the bleachers were staring straight at me.

The ball came fast. I didn't even have time to think about it. I just watched it closely, put out my glove, and made a *perfect* catch!

Hmmm, I thought, maybe this isn't going to be so tough, after all. A crowd might be just the thing I need to bring out the best in me.

"Okay, Alex," shouted my coach, again, "here comes another one."

This time it was a hard grounder. As soon as I saw it coming, I ran up to it, bent down, and scooped it up into my glove.

"All right out there, Frankovitch," yelled the coach. "Way to play!"

Boy, was he ever proud of me! The day was turning out a whole lot better than I thought.

chapter ten

The umpire blew his whistle. It was time for the big game to begin.

Our team ran in from the field. On the sideline T.J. was being interviewed for the six o'clock news. I tried to get close enough to listen to what they were saying, but they had just finished. As T.J. walked off, I heard the newsman say, "Good luck out there today, T.J. We're all rooting for you!"

I looked into the bleachers. On the front row sat Fran and Ethel. They were a little bit hard to spot because they didn't have their mops with them. I smiled to myself. Not *everyone's* rooting for you, T.J., I thought.

The umpire's whistle blew again. "Teams take the field!" he shouted.

T.J.'s team ran out to the field. Naturally, T.J. was pitching. He started warming up and, just like in our contest, every ball he threw went zinging over the plate at about sixty miles an hour. I hate to keep saying this, but he really *was* the best Little League pitcher I had ever seen. I sure was glad I didn't have to be up first.

"Batter up!" shouted the ump.

Kevin Murphy was the first batter on our team. As soon as he stepped up to the plate, I could tell he was really nervous. He kept trying to spit, but nothing would come out. Instead, he just kept making this funny sound with his lips. He looked ridiculous.

When T.J. looked at Kevin, he smiled. Then he wound up and threw the ball as hard as he could. Kevin never even saw it go by.

"Steerrriiiikkkee one!" yelled the umpire.

Kevin looked confused. "Did he already throw one?"

T.J. just laughed and went into his windup for his second pitch. This time he threw it a little bit slower. Kevin swung with all his might. But just as the ball got to the plate, it curved.

"Steerrriiiikkkee two!" screamed the umpire

again. Poor Kevin hadn't even come close. I *really* felt sorry for him. Whenever you swing as hard as you can and miss it, you always feel like an idiot. Kevin tried acting tough but, when he went to spit again, he just made that same stupid sound with his lips.

Quickly, he took his bat back and got ready for the next pitch. But unfortunately, the third ball that T.J. threw was even better than the first two. Kevin just watched it go streaking by.

"Strike three! Batter's out!" yelled the ump.

Everyone in the stands began to cheer loudly for T.J. Kevin sat down on the bench and began to cry. He couldn't seem to stop. After a while, his mother had to be called out of the bleachers to get him calmed down. At first the whole team was pretty embarrassed about it. But as it turned out, Kevin was the best batter of the inning. He was the only one who swung.

The second batter, Willy Jenson, didn't even *try* to swing. And by the time the third batter got up, he was so nervous, he didn't even bother to put the bat up to his shoulder. He just stood there, let three pitches go by, and sat down.

Our team was out in the field before we knew it. Everyone was looking pretty sad. What we really needed was a pep talk to get the old team spirit going. So I called all the guys into a huddle.

"Okay, you guys," I said, trying to act real peppy. "All we need to do is hold them. What do you say? Let's get them out one-two-three! Three up. Three down!"

The first baseman looked at me and laughed right out loud. "Frankovitch, you jerk," he said, "who do you think you're kidding? Our team hasn't made three outs in a row all year!"

"Yeah, Alex," said the catcher. "We're lucky if we make three outs the whole game. So why don't you just shut up and get out to center field where you belong?"

So much for the old team spirit. But I didn't care what they said. I was going to cheer our team on, whether they wanted me to or not.

Frankie Rogers was going to be our starting pitcher. As I walked out to center field, I watched him warm up. He threw twice and said he was ready. Frankie doesn't like to warm up for too long. He only throws a couple of good balls a game, and he doesn't want to risk throwing them in practice.

I started cheering. "Okay, Frankie, pitch it in there, babe. Right over the plate, Frankie! You can do it!"

Frankie threw the first ball. It hit the dirt about ten feet in front of the plate.

"Ball one!" shouted the umpire.

"That's okay, Frankie, don't worry. You can do it, babe!" I yelled.

All of a sudden Frankie asked the umpire for time-out. Then he turned and walked out toward center field. At first I figured he was probably coming out to thank me for cheering. But when he got close enough, I could see he wasn't smiling. I walked up to meet him.

"Will you please shut up, Alex?" he screamed. "You're really getting on my nerves! How in the world am I supposed to concentrate with all that shouting going on out here?"

"That's not shouting, Frankie, that's cheering!" I told him. "I'm just trying to encourage you a little bit."

"Yeah well, if you ask me, you're acting like a jerk. So how about just shutting up?" Frankie said, stomping back to the pitcher's mound.

As he got ready to throw his next pitch, I yelled, "Okay, Frankie, throw any dumb kind of pitch you want. See if *I* care!"

The ball zoomed toward the plate but, unfortunately, it was just a little bit low. It hit the batter on the foot and he took his base. The next batter hurried up to the plate. Once again, Frankie got ready. This time, he hit the kid at bat in the arm.

If you ask me, he was embarrassing the whole

team. It was bad enough that he couldn't pitch. But to make matters worse, he didn't even throw the ball hard enough to hurt anyone.

I looked over to the sidelines. The news camera was rolling. "Oh no!" I said to myself. I put both my hands over my face so that no one would recognize me on the six o'clock news.

While I was standing there with my face covered up, I heard a big loud crack. I looked up. Some kid had hit the ball and was running to first base.

Everyone began to holler and scream. Then, all the guys on my team turned to look at me. At first I wasn't sure why, so I just sort of smiled. But suddenly I realized that they were watching to see if I was going to catch the ball which was probably headed my way. I panicked. I didn't even know where the ball was! I looked up into the sky to try and find it, but I couldn't see it anywhere! The worst feeling in the world is knowing that any minute a hard ball is going to smack you right in the head, and you don't know where it's coming from.

I had to try to protect myself. Quickly I took my glove off my hand and put it on my head. It was just in time! I felt something hit my glove with a big thud! I felt it roll off the top of my head and land on the ground next to me.

My team started going crazy. "Oh no! He dropped it! He dropped the stupid ball!" they screamed.

"I did not!" I screamed back at them. "How can a person drop something when he didn't even catch it in the first place? Just because something lands on your head does not mean that you caught it!"

"It does too!" shouted the third baseman. "You caught it on your head, and then dropped it!"

"If a bird poops on your head, you don't say that you've caught it, do you, you jerk?" I yelled back.

I was so busy arguing that I forgot all about the ball. By the time I remembered, it was too late. Three runs had already scored.

The coach was waving at me from the sidelines. Just to be polite, I waved back.

"He's not waving, Frankovitch, you jerk," shouted the left fielder. "He's shaking his fists!"

I looked closer. Yup. Those were fists, all right. He was even madder than I thought.

It took a few minutes for things to settle back down. Frankie got ready to face his fourth batter. I looked to see who was up. My heart began to pound.

Slowly T.J. walked up to the plate and took a few practice swings. Then he knocked the dirt off his shoes and pointed to me in center field. My stomach started doing flips. Oh no, I thought to myself. He's going to slam it right to me! Nervously, I backed up. If I made another mistake out there, I was doomed.

Frankie pitched the ball. T.J. pulled the bat back and hit it with all his might. It was a hard grounder, and just as I thought, headed my way!

I watched it as it bounced over second base and started into center field. If only I could remember what the coach had told me about catching hard grounders! If only I could get T. J. Stoner out!

I tried to do everything just like in the big leagues. First, I ran up to meet the ball. Then, I stooped down directly in front of it. I even kept my eye on it. It's almost here! I thought. I've got it! I've got it!

But just as it was about to roll into my glove, it hit a small dirt mound and took a crazy bounce to the right.

"Oh no!" I screamed. I made a diving leap trying to stop it, but it was no use. The ball sped away and kept right on rolling all the way to the back fence.

The crowd went wild. I looked at T.J. as he

was running the bases. He saw me and tipped his cap. What a big shot! He really made me sick!

My coach was screaming for me to get the ball. But I was just too mad. "He hit it!" I hollered, pointing at T.J. "Let *him* go get it!"

Finally, the left fielder went out to retrieve the ball. My coach's face got so red, I could see it from center field. For a minute there, I actually thought he might blow up. Boy, was I in trouble now. I figured it might be a good time to have another little chat with God.

"God, please, whatever you do, don't let our team get up to bat again until my coach settles down. If I have to go over there now, he's going to kill me, God, I know he will. And if you think I'm a problem down here, just imagine what it would be like to have me running around heaven with you. You'd never have a minute's peace, God. Think about it."

Right after I finished talking to God, I watched as Frankie threw nine straight strikes in a row!

"I've done something to upset you, haven't I, God?" I said, looking up to the sky. Then I thought a minute. "If you're still mad about me wearing a gorilla costume in the Christmas play, it wasn't my fault. I told my teacher at least fifty

82

times that I did *not* want to be one of those sheep in the manger."

All the kids on my team were passing me as they headed for the bench. I saw the coach waiting for me on the sideline. He had a very strange grin on his face and kept pounding his fist into his hand. As I walked by, he grabbed my arm and handed me a bat.

I forced a smile. "Someday we'll look back on this and laugh," I said quietly.

"Yeah, Frankovitch," he growled, his teeth clenched together. "You and I are going to do a whole lot of laughing right after the game. But right now you're up. So get your tail over there." Then he gave me a little shove toward home plate.

I dropped my glove on the ground and looked around as I headed toward the batter's box. Sitting in the stands, Fran and Ethel were clapping. Standing on the sideline, the cameraman was filming. And waiting on the mound in front of me, T. J. Stoner was grinning.

This was easily the worst moment of my life. There was no escape. No joke would save me now.

"Get going, Alex!" screamed my coach from behind me.

I gulped and stepped up to the plate. T.J.

began to laugh. Then he turned around and hollered to the rest of his team.

"Easy out! Easy out!" He screamed loud enough for the whole world to hear.

All the guys in the infield took four giant steps in. That didn't do much for my confidence.

"Get ready for a bunt!" yelled T.J.

Oh wonderful! I thought to myself. Now everyone knows exactly what I'm going to do. But I didn't really have a choice. It was either bunt or not hit it at all.

T.J. threw his first pitch. Whoosh! I couldn't believe how fast it came streaking over the plate!

"Steerrriiiikkkee one!" shouted the umpire.

Why do umpires always have to yell "strike" so loud? Whenever it's a ball they practically whisper. But as soon as they see a strike, they act like everyone's deaf or something.

I made up my mind that I wasn't going to just stand there like an idiot and let another ball go by. If I was going to strike out, I was going to do it swinging.

T.J. wound up and threw again. Quickly, I stuck out my bat. As the ball whizzed over the plate, it hit the bat on the corner and began rolling toward first base.

I couldn't believe it. I started running as fast

as I could. If only I could get on base. I'd be a hero! And no one can be mad at a hero. Not even my coach.

The first baseman ran toward me to pick up the ball. Meanwhile, T.J. ran over to cover first.

Everyone was going crazy. My coach was jumping up and down as I passed him running to first. He didn't even look mad anymore. I just had to make it!

The first baseman picked up the ball and got ready to make the throw. I was almost there. Just three more steps to go.

He threw. T.J. got ready for the catch. I had to do something!

"BOOGA BOOGA!" I screamed suddenly, flinging my arms all around. "BOOGA BOOGA!"

T.J. looked surprised. And for just a split second he took his eye off the ball. It shot past him and rolled into the outfield. I WAS SAFE!

As the outfielders scrambled for the ball, I took a chance and headed for second.

"Legs, don't fail me now!" I yelled as I hit full speed. I didn't look back until I was safe at second.

The crowd in the stands went wild.

"I did it! I did it!" I screamed. "A double! I got a double!"

The second baseman told me to shut up. But I ignored him. No one could ruin this moment for me, not the second baseman, not T. J. Stoner, not anyone!

But something didn't look quite right. From second base, I watched as T.J.'s coach ran onto the field and began arguing with the umpire. And before I knew it, my coach was out there, too.

I couldn't figure out what the problem could be. The whole thing was so simple. T.J. had missed the ball and I got a double. A double! Wow! I still couldn't believe it. I started jumping up and down all over again.

Out in the field, my coach had started jumping up and down right along with me. But for some reason he didn't look very happy. All of a sudden, I saw the umpire begin to walk out toward second base.

Don't panic, Alex, I thought. Maybe he's not really coming to second base at all. Maybe during all that excitement, someone threw toilet paper streamers onto the outfield and the umpire's walking out there to clean them up. But in a few seconds, the umpire was standing next to me at second base.

He leaned right down in my face and screamed, "You're out!"

"Out?" I asked, puzzled. "How could I be out? I bunted!"

"You interfered with the play at first base," he said.

"I did not!" I argued. "I didn't even touch T.J.!"

"You jumped up and down and shouted 'booga booga,'" said the umpire.

My coach ran up behind the umpire and held out his rule book. "Show me where it says you can't say 'booga booga!'" he demanded. "Tell me, huh? What page is the 'no booga booga' rule on?"

I don't know why, but suddenly this whole conversation seemed pretty funny. I looked up at the umpire and smiled. "Booga booga," I said quietly.

"Get off the field, you smart aleck," he ordered.

I nodded my head. "Booga," I said again softly.

Then, slowly I began trotting off the field toward the bench. As I was running, I could see T.J. out of the corner of my eye. He had started to laugh. Only I knew he wasn't laughing *with* me. He was laughing *at* me.

I just couldn't let him get away with it. Suddenly, I got an idea. If T.J. wanted to laugh, I might as well give him something to laugh about.

Quickly, I changed my direction and began running right toward him. When he looked up and saw me coming, he stopped laughing. I guess he wasn't quite sure what kind of crazy thing I was going to do next.

When I got to the pitcher's mound, I jumped up and down a couple of times, then quickly lifted up his arm and started tickling him. "Booga booga," I said, poking at his ribs.

For the first time in his life, T.J. looked embarrassed. It was great while it lasted, but unfortunately, it didn't last too long. After a couple of seconds he began to look extremely angry. That's when I decided to split.

I ran off the field as fast as I could, and then out the gate. I didn't slow down until I was safely in my own room. Locking the door behind me, I had a feeling that I wouldn't want to come out for a long, long time.

chapter eleven

I stayed in my room for about an hour before I heard my parents come home from the game. I had pushed my dresser over in front of the door so that no one could get in. I wasn't sure exactly what my father was going to do when he got home, but I had a pretty good idea.

I figured he would probably knock on my door and tell me he wanted to talk to me. When I let him in, he would sit down on the bed and just stare at me for a while. Then he would start one of those big "talks" that parents love to have with their children, and that children hate to have with their parents.

He would start off by telling me that running

away from a problem never solves anything. Then he would say that he hoped I wouldn't keep trying to make a big joke out of everything I'm not good at. And he would end up by telling me that "no matter what you try to do in life, you must always try to do the best you can." Then he would ask me if I understood what he was trying to tell me.

"Yes," I would answer, "I think that you're trying to tell me never to do anything stupid to embarrass the family again."

Then my father would stare at me for a minute, shake his head, and start out of my room. On his way out he would probably mutter something like, "I might as well be talking to a brick wall."

All of a sudden I heard the back door open and close. My heart started to pound. I listened to the sound of Dad's footsteps coming down the hall.

Here it comes, I thought to myself. Next he's going to knock on my door and tell me that he wants to have a little talk.

Knock, knock, knock. . . .

"Who is it?" I asked, as if I didn't know.

"It's Dad."

"Dad who?"

"Come on, Alex," said my father. "Open the door. I want to talk to you a minute."

"I already know what you want, Dad," I replied. "You want to talk to me about what happened today. And you probably even think that by talking it out, you can make me feel better. But you might as well save your breath, Dad. It's no use. The way I feel, no one in the whole world could make me feel better. So if you don't mind, I've decided to become a hermit and live right here in my room for the rest of my life. If you or Mom would just shove a bologna sandwich under the door every once in a while, I'd really appreciate it.

"And one more thing, Dad," I added. "Don't try and force your way in here to try and save me. I shoved my dresser up against the door, and I wouldn't want you to hurt yourself."

I figured that by this time, my father was really feeling sorry for me.

"Well, Dad," I said, "it's been real nice having you for a father. I'll see you when I'm all grown up."

I heard my father leave my door and walk back down the hall toward the kitchen. I knew he was probably going to tell my mother what had happened. Then the two of them would sit down together and try to figure out a way to get me to come out.

A few minutes later, I heard a noise at my door. Aha! I thought to myself. There they are now! They're probably going to stand there and beg me to come out!

But something behind the dresser was making a funny sound. When I looked to see what it was, I saw a bologna sandwich in a plastic bag, being squeezed underneath the space at the bottom of my door.

"Very funny, Dad!" I yelled. "Very, very funny!"

I grabbed the flattened sandwich and threw it in my trash can. Parents! Just when you think you've got them all figured out, they go and pull a dumb trick like that.

The next day was Sunday. And, except for a few minutes while my parents were at church, I didn't come out of my room all day long.

The thing that bothered me most about staying in there all day was that my parents didn't seem to care at all. In fact, every once in a while, I could even hear them laughing. What kind of people think it's funny for a kid to spend the rest of his life shut away in a tiny bedroom?

The other thing that bothered me was how boring it was. Most of the time I just lay on my bed. There were probably better things to be doing, but just in case someone looked through the window to see me, I didn't want it to seem like I was having a good time.

By dinner time, I was really wanting to come out. I could hear my mother starting to make dinner in the kitchen. Boy, was I ever hungry! I had hardly eaten a thing all day.

While my parents were at church I had snuck a few snacks and a couple of apples, but it wasn't nearly enough to keep a growing boy going. Besides, all I had left were two pretzels and one broken graham cracker. I tried putting the pretzels between the graham cracker pieces to make a sandwich, but it looked terrible.

Being hungry wasn't my biggest problem, though. I had to go to the bathroom worse than I've ever had to go in my whole entire life. I waited as long as I could, but finally, I just couldn't stand it one more minute. I pushed the dresser away from the door and ran to the bathroom. I know my parents must have heard me, but no one even bothered to walk down the hall to see how I was. On the way back to my room, I heard them sitting down to dinner. I could smell the delicious aroma all the way down the hall.

I began to wonder how long a person could go without food before he passed out and died. The thought made me very nervous. My stomach started to growl loudly. I decided that maybe if I just got a little peek at some real food, it might make me feel better.

Quietly, I tiptoed down the hall toward the kitchen. Just one little peek . . . that's all I wanted. I stopped at the kitchen door and got down on my hands and knees. Slowly, I peeked around the corner.

Fried chicken and corn on the cob. I just couldn't stand it! My mouth had begun to water so much that I almost started drooling down the front of my shirt.

My parents were staring at me. Neither one of them said anything. They kept right on eating!

"Listen, Mom and Dad," I said, "you might as well forget trying to pretend I'm not here. I know you can see me."

My father looked up. "You're the one who doesn't want anyone to bother you, Alex," he said. "It wasn't our idea."

"Well, maybe I've changed my mind," I said, staring at all the corn on the cob, piled high in a bowl in the middle of the table. Butter was melting down the sides. I sat down in my chair.

"Chicken?" asked my father.

"I am not!" I shouted angrily. "Just because I ran off the Little League field doesn't mean I'm a chicken!"

My father gave me a real disgusted look and then just shook his head. "Chicken?" he said to my mother as he picked up the plate and handed it to her.

"Yes, please," said my mother as she took a big piece of fried chicken off the plate.

My father turned to me and said, "Shall we try it again, Alex? Chicken?" Then he passed me the plate.

I managed to mumble "thank you" but that was the last word I said the entire meal.

My parents tried to talk to me about what happened at the game, but I just couldn't do it. It's bad enough when you act like an idiot, but it's even worse when you have to talk about it.

After dinner, I went back to my room and fed the rest of the graham cracker and the pretzels to my fish. Then I got my pajamas on and went straight to bed. I knew that my parents would make me go to school the next day, and I was going to need a lot of energy to face the kids in my class.

chapter twelve

One of the things I really hate about my mother
is that she always seems to know when I'm lying.
Don't ask me how she does it. I've tried to figure
it out, but so far I've had no luck at all.

On Monday morning, when she came into my
room to get me out of bed, I started moaning
and groaning and holding my sides.

"Ohhhh . . ." I wailed, "my stomach, my
stomach."

My mother rolled up my window shade.
"What a nice sunny day out there," she said
cheerfully.

"Ohhhh!" I cried loudly, trying to get her
attention. "I'm not kidding, Mom. It really hurts!
I think I'm dying."

"Okay, Alex," she said standing at the end of my bed with her arms crossed. "If you want me to play this little game with you . . . fine. Now I guess I'm supposed to ask you what's wrong with your stomach."

"Aaggg," I said, doubling over in pain. "It must have been something I ate. Maybe there was something wrong with the chicken I had last night for dinner."

My mother casually strolled over to my dresser and looked down into my fish bowl. "Did your fish have chicken for dinner, too?" she asked.

"Don't try to make me laugh, Mom," I said. "It hurts too much."

"I'm not trying to make you laugh, Alex," said my mother. "Your fish is dead."

"Oh no!" I shouted. I jumped out of bed and ran over to the goldfish bowl. "He's not dead! He can't be!"

"Maybe he's just trying to learn how to float on his back," said my mother with a little laugh.

"How can you make a joke about this?" I hollered.

"Oh, for heaven's sake, Alex," she answered, "you've only had that fish for four days. Your fish never last more than a week. How much can a four-day-old fish mean to you? I would think that by this time, you'd be used to them dying. So far this month, you've already overfed five of them."

"It doesn't matter. I still don't think that you should make fun of someone's pet dying," I insisted.

I got my little fish net and scooped up my dead fish. Then I ran him into the bathroom and flushed him down the toilet. When I got back to my room, my mother was standing there with a smile on her face.

"I see that your stomach is better," she said. "You haven't moaned or groaned for several minutes."

"Ohhhh," I said quickly, grabbing my sides and bending over.

"Forget it, Alex. It won't work. Get dressed. You're going to school," she said, leaving the room.

"I blew it!" I said to myself. I almost had her believing me and I blew it. If it wasn't for that stupid fish, I wouldn't have had to go to school. Boy, you try to do your pet a favor by giving him a special dessert, and this is how he thanks you. He dies. What a pal.

On the way to school, I tried to plan what I would say to the kids when I got there. I knew that everyone was going to be making fun of the way that I had acted at the game. And what made it even worse was that I also knew that T. J. Stoner was going to be the big fat hero.

As I got near the playground, I could already see about a million kids gathered around T.J. They were asking him for his autograph! All those jerky kids were actually asking T. J. Stoner for his autograph!

I rushed by in a hurry to get to my classroom. Luckily, no one saw me. I figured that if I could just get to my desk before class started, no one would have a chance to make fun of me.

I was wrong. When I walked into the classroom, my teacher looked up and started to giggle. "Ooga ooga," she said.

I frowned. "It wasn't ooga ooga,' Mrs. Grayson," I said disgustedly. "'Ooga ooga' is the sound an old-fashioned car makes. What I *said* was, 'booga booga.'"

"Oh," she said quietly, looking a little embarrassed. "It was hard to hear you from the stands."

"Mrs. Grayson, I was wondering if I could sit in the back of the room today?" I asked. "I'm feeling a little sick and I might need to run to the bathroom from time to time."

Before Mrs. Grayson had a chance to answer me, the bell rang and everyone started rushing in to take their seats.

"Hey, look who's here," shouted T.J. "It's Booga Booga Frankovitch!" The whole class started laughing at once.

"Would you like to go to the nurse?" Mrs. Grayson shouted over the laughter.

"No thanks," I yelled even louder. "If I feel like I'm going to toss my cookies, I'll just aim for T.J. He's a pretty good catch."

"What a threat!" laughed T.J. "If you toss your cookies like you toss a baseball, you'll miss me by a mile."

"That's enough," said Mrs. Grayson, motioning for both of us to sit down.

I was glad she stepped in. For the first time in my life, I didn't have anything else to say.

T.J. raised his hand. "Mrs. Grayson," he said after he was called on, "would it be all right if I finished signing a couple of autographs for some of the kids in the room? I didn't have a chance to finish before class."

Mrs. Grayson smiled. "Sure, T.J.," she answered. "I think we can spare a few minutes to let the National Little League Champion sign a few autographs."

Everyone started clapping. I couldn't believe it! You might have thought he was Tom Seaver or something!

"Boys and girls," said Mrs. Grayson, "I really think that we're very fortunate to have T.J. in our room this year. In case any of you missed it on the news Saturday night, T. J. Stoner is going to be in the *Guinness Book of World Records*! He now holds the record for the most games ever won in a row in the history of Little League baseball!"

More applause.

I couldn't stand it one more minute. Quickly I got out my notebook and scribbled a message to Brian. It read:

> Say something nice about me and I'll give you a dollar after school.

Brian's hand shot up in the air like a bullet. Brian loves money more than any kid I know.

"Yes, Brian?" said Mrs. Grayson.

"Mrs. Grayson," he began, "I think we're also fortunate to have Alex Frankovitch in our class this year. If you ask me, it takes a very special person to stand in front of a crowd and make a big buffoon out of himself like Alex did."

This time even Mrs Grayson couldn't keep from laughing. When I become popular, I think Brian will be the first friend I'll dump.

The rest of the day I tried to stay as quiet as I could. I wanted to make it as easy as possible for people to ignore me. But it didn't work. All day long, whenever anyone walked by my desk, they would lean over and whisper "booga booga" in my ear as they passed. Then they'd walk away and laugh as if they were the first one to think of it.

By one o'clock I just couldn't take it one more second. That's when Harold Marshall raised his hand and asked if he could sharpen his pencil. Harold's a troublemaker, so he has to ask permission to do anything.

Mrs. Grayson nodded her head and Harold started up my row to the pencil sharpener. I was positive that when he passed my desk he would try to get in a couple of quick boogas. So as he got closer to my seat, I got ready for him.

Just as Harold leaned over to whisper in my ear, I quickly turned my face in his direction, making it look as if he had just leaned over and kissed me

I jumped up. "Yuck! Did you see that?" I yelled wiping off my face. "Harold Marshall just kissed me on the cheek! How revolting!"

Harold started turning red. "I did not!" he sputtered.

"Then how did my cheek get so wet?" I asked,

pointing to my face. "Mrs. Grayson, can I go to the bathroom and wash it off? I think I'm allergic to slobber."

Mrs. Grayson motioned me out the door and ordered Harold to sit down. As I left the room, I saw several kids covering their faces as Harold passed by.

Unfortunately, making a fool out of Harold didn't really change anything. As soon as I got back from the bathroom, the booga boogas started all over again.

I looked at the clock. Only forty-five minutes to go. I just didn't know if I could make it that long. I began feeling sorry for myself. It seemed like nothing I had ever done had turned out right. Even when I did something well, like bunting for instance, it turned out wrong.

"Let's face it, Alex," I finally said to myself, "the only thing that you've ever really succeeded at is being short. You're a nothing. A big fat nothing!"

I leaned my head down and rested it on my desk. I felt my eyes starting to get wet. Oh terrific! I thought. Now big fat nothing Alex Frankovitch is going to cry in front of the whole class.

Suddenly, I heard my name being called. I

didn't look up. "*Alex Frankovitch?*" said the voice again. But it wasn't my teacher. Quickly I wiped a tear out of my eye and looked up. The voice was coming from the loudspeaker on the wall.

It was our principal, Mr. Vernon. "*Mrs. Grayson, is Alex Frankovitch there?*" he asked.

"Yes he is, Mr. Vernon," she answered. "Would you like me to send him down to your office?"

"*No,*" said Mr. Vernon. "*I have an announcement to make about him and I just wanted to be sure that he was there.*"

My heart started beating wildly. T.J. pointed at me and started to laugh. We both figured we knew what was coming. Mr. Vernon was going to make a couple more booga-booga jokes so the whole school could have a good laugh.

Mr. Vernon clicked on the loudspeaker so that all the other classrooms could hear him.

"*Attention, boys and girls, may I have your attention, please?*

"*First of all, I'd like to congratulate T. J. Stoner on his brilliant Little League performance! The entire school is very, very proud of him. I think that we should all give him a big round of applause!*"

Then he stopped a minute so that all the classrooms could clap.

"By the way," he continued, *"I have already spoken to T.J. today, and he has agreed to stay after school in case any of you would like to stop by and get his autograph. We'll have a table set up for him in the Multipurpose Room."*

T.J. just sat there and grinned like a big shot. I wished I had my dead fish back. I would have put it down his shirt.

"Now then," Mr. Vernon's voice came back through the loudspeaker. *"There's someone else in Mrs. Grayson's sixth-grade room that I'd also like to congratulate."*

Here it comes, I thought to myself. He's going to congratulate me for being the biggest buffoon in the school.

"It seems that Alex Frankovitch has also made quite a name for himself."

I could feel everyone's eyes staring at my back. A few kids were already giggling. Tears started to fill my eyes again, but I forced them back into my head.

"I have just received news from his mother, that today Alex Frankovitch got a letter in the mail announcing that he is the winner of the National Kitty Fritters Television Contest! And according to the letter, as his prize, Alex will get to appear in a national television commercial!

"Congratulations, Alex! We're all very excited about having one of our students become a big TV star!"

The whole class was completely silent. No one could believe what Mr. Vernon had said. Especially me! I only wrote that letter as a joke!

After a few seconds I guess the shock wore off, and everyone started clapping. Mrs. Grayson told me to stand up and take a bow, but my legs were so weak I couldn't get out of my chair. So I just turned around and waved instead.

Just then, my mother appeared in the doorway. Mrs. Grayson went to greet her and called me to the front of the room.

"How was that for a big surprise?" asked my mother when she saw me. "I was going to tell you in person, but I happened to see Mr. Vernon on the way down the hall, and we decided it might be more fun to surprise you with it over the loudspeaker. Were you surprised?"

I nodded. Up until this time, I had been unable to say anything. It's hard to form words when your mouth is hanging wide open.

"When do you get to do the commercial?" asked Mrs. Grayson.

"I'm not sure," I said finally, trying to think back to the instructions on the contest sheet. "I just entered that contest as a joke," I admitted. "I didn't really pay much attention to the prize."

My mother waved a piece of paper in front of my face. "It says here that the commercial will be made in New York sometime within the next six months!" she said proudly. "They also said that your contest entry was the funniest, most original essay that they had ever received. And they can't wait to meet you!"

Mrs. Grayson put her hand on my shoulder. "This might just be your start in show business!" she said. Then she and my mother both laughed.

Well I hate to tell them, but they just might be right. Once those Kitty Fritters people get ahold of me, they'll probably never want to let me go. I smiled at the thought of it.

After a few more minutes, my mother left the classroom and went home. Since the day was almost over, Mrs. Grayson told us to put all our work away.

"I just got a great idea," she said. "Why don't we have our two class celebrities come up here and answer questions like they do on TV?"

Since I was already in the front of the room, I casually got up from my seat and sat down on the front edge of Mrs. Grayson's desk. T.J. was a little slower getting there. But finally he shuffled up and sat down next to me. I could tell he really hated sharing his big day with me.

"Okay," said Mrs. Grayson. "Who has questions?"

Harold Marshall's hand was up like a bullet.

"Yes, Harold?" said T.J. quickly.

Harold stood up. "I have a question for Alex," he said, laughing. T.J. smiled. I was sure he already knew what Harold was going to ask. They had probably set it up before T.J. came to the front of the room.

"What exactly is a booga booga?" he asked, cracking up.

I knew it! I knew he was going to say something like that!

I thought a minute before I answered. "It's hard to explain," I said after a minute. "A booga booga is sort of a big wad of green slimy . . . wait a minute! What a coincidence! If everyone will turn around quickly, there's a booga booga sitting in Harold's hair right now!"

Everybody started laughing all at once. Everybody except Harold, that is. Mrs. Grayson didn't seem to mind. I guess she knew that Harold deserved it.

After that, Harold didn't give me any more trouble and T.J. and I started answering questions. Melissa Phillips asked each of us who our most famous relative was. T.J. said it was his brother, Matt Stoner. I said it was my grandmother, Steve Garvey.

Most of the questions were about the *Guinness Book of World Records*. But I didn't really mind. It felt good just sitting up there.

I looked over at T.J. as he answered a question from Adam Brooks. T.J. was a creep all right. But maybe it wasn't all his fault. I had a feeling that being a big shot can make a creep out of anyone if they're not careful. Even a wonderful guy like me. Maybe I better not dump Brian after all, I thought to myself. It might be bad for my image.

"That's all we have time for today," said Mrs. Grayson. "If we have any free time tomorrow, we can continue."

I went to my desk and picked up my homework books. After the bell rang, I filed out of the room with everyone else. As I passed by Mrs. Grayson, she patted me on the back. Maybe after all these years I'd finally done it. Maybe I'd finally found a teacher who liked my sense of humor.

Outside the building, Brian was waiting for me. When he saw me coming, he smiled. I didn't.

"Oh no you don't," I said. "Just because I'm famous and popular doesn't mean you can come crawling back to me. I'm not forgetting how you called me a buffoon."

Brian got a puzzled look on his face. "What are you talking about, Alex?" he asked. "Who's crawling back? I'm just waiting to collect the buck you promised me for saying something nice."

"You call buffoon, nice?"

"I didn't call you a buffoon, Alex," he corrected. "If I had called you a buffoon I would have only charged you fifty cents. I called you a *big* buffoon. That's a dollar. You get twice the buffoon for your money."

I couldn't keep myself from laughing. It's hard to stay mad at Brian. We started walking home together. As we walked, a couple of kids congratulated me on the TV commercial. No one asked for an autograph, but I figure that will probably come later.

On the way home, Brian and I talked a lot about my future as a comedian. We decided that as long as I've already gotten my first break into show business, I might as well go on to become disgustingly rich. I told Brian that I would think about letting him write some of my material. "Material" is the word comedians use when they talk about their jokes.

I still can't get over it. Me, skinny little Alex Frankovitch, a star. Hmm. I wonder if the Kitty Fritters people will want me to read my winning essay on the commercial. No, they'll probably just want to use my cute little face smiling at a cat food bag or something. I just hope they don't want me to do anything dumb. Sometimes these commercials can get pretty crazy.

One time I saw a cereal commercial where they made this little kid dress up like a raisin and dance around a big bowl of oatmeal. Boy, the thought of doing something like that really gives me the creeps. Hmm. Maybe it's time for another little chat.

"Hello, God? It's Alex Frankovitch again. Listen, I have another little favor I'd like to ask. As you probably know I'm going to be on a TV commercial soon. And well, I'd *really* appreciate it if I didn't have to dress up like a Kitty Fritter and dance around a cat dish. I mean, I don't mind making a fool of myself once in a while, God. But I do have my pride.

"Are you listening, God? If you are, please just do me this one little favor, and I promise to stop singing 'doo-da' at the end of the hymns in church, and start singing 'Amen' like everyone else. How's that? Is it a deal, God? If it is, show me by making the wind start blowing.

111

"Aha! I saw it. I saw a little leaf move on that tree over there. Thanks a lot, God! I *knew* I could count on you.

"And remember, if you ever need a favor, you can count on me, too. Just look me up in New York or Hollywood.

"I'll be in the Yellow Pages under 'Star.'"

BARBARA PARK is one of today's funniest, most popular writers for middle graders. Her novels, which include *Skinnybones, The Kid in the Red Jacket, Maxie, Rosie, and Earl—Partners in Grime,* and *Rosie Swanson: Fourth-Grade Geek for President,* have won just about every award given by children.

She has also created the Junie B. Jones character for the Random House First Stepping Stone list. Recent books about Junie include *Junie B. Jones and Some Sneaky Peeky Spying* and *Junie B. Jones and Her Big Fat Mouth.*

Ms. Park earned a B.S. degree in education at the University of Alabama and lives in Paradise Valley, Arizona, with her husband.

It was his big break...or was it?

ALMOST STARRING SKINNYBONES

by Barbara Park

When Alex Frankovitch—better known as Skinnybones—gets the chance to star in a TV commercial, it seems as though his dreams have come true. Who cares if it's just a cat food commercial and he plays a six-year-old wearing a dorky coonskin cap? It's still national television—and a rare opportunity to thumb his nose at his classmates. So why does the Alex Frankovitch Fan Club attract only two members—a cat and a toddler? And why do all the kids laugh hysterically every time they see him? Is this the end of Skinnybones' career as a Big Celebrity?

"Park is laugh-out-loud funny!"   —*Booklist*

"Once again demonstrating her remarkable ear for dialogue, Park also shows a good sense of timing in this fast-paced outing."

—*School Library Journal*

A BULLSEYE BOOK PUBLISHED BY RANDOM HOUSE, INC.